"Somebody p
Jason said.

"But—that would have killed me." Ava couldn't get the image of her charred car from her mind.

The captain met her eyes for just a moment. Instead of hardened anger in his flintlike gray eyes, she saw a hint of sympathy, maybe even apology.

The change shook her as much as the realization that she'd narrowly escaped a horrific end. "They wanted me dead? But why?"

Jason offered her his hand and pulled her up to a seated position. He looked her full in the face, a bit of sadness shimmering in his steel-gray eyes. "Do you have any enemies?"

Ava stared at him for long seconds. Finally she answered, "You?"

"I'm the worst enemy you have?" he asked.

She nodded, no longer trusting her voice.

"Then I don't know why anyone would put a bomb in your car." He sucked in a sharp breath and met her eyes again. "But I intend to find out."

Books by Rachelle McCalla

RACHELLE McCALLA

is a mild-mannered housewife, and the toughest she ever has to get is when she's trying to keep her four kids quiet in church. Though she often gets in over her head, as her characters do, and has to find a way out, her adventures have more to do with sorting out the car pool and providing food for the potluck. She's never been arrested, gotten in a fistfight or been shot at. And she'd like to keep it that way! For recipes, fun background notes on the places and characters in this book and more information on forthcoming titles, visit www.rachellemccalla.com.

ROYAL WEDDING THREAT

RACHELLE MCCALLA

HARLEQUIN® LOVE INSPIRED® SUSPENSE

Recycling programs
for this product may
not exist in your area.

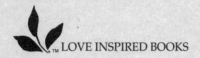

™ LOVE INSPIRED BOOKS

ISBN-13: 978-0-373-44584-4

ROYAL WEDDING THREAT

Copyright © 2014 by Rachelle McCalla

Though one may be overpowered,
two can defend themselves. A cord of three strands
is not quickly broken.
—*Ecclesiastes* 4:12

To Ray, always

ONE

"Ms. Wright? Ms. Wright, wait!"

Ava Wright did not wait, but trotted toward the pedestrian gate at the rear of the palace complex as quickly as she dared in her three-inch heels. She made eye contact with the guard inside the gatehouse and gave him her best commanding glare, signaling that she wanted the exit unlocked immediately.

The green light signaled that the gate's electronic lock had been momentarily deactivated, allowing her to open the gate and pass through. Ava felt a small shiver of satisfaction as she made her escape. Good. Jason Selini might be the head of the Lydian Royal Guard, but she could still get her way, even if it meant giving orders to his men.

But the captain of the royal guard was right behind her. "We need to discuss this further, Ms. Wright. Our conversation isn't over!" Captain Selini was one of the few people Ava had met who could match her commanding tone note for note, glare for glare.

No way was she butting heads with him any more today. The man was impossibly stubborn and could be completely unreasonable once he'd made up his mind on an issue—and he'd already made it clear that morning that his mind was quite made up about her plans for Princess Anastasia's wedding.

Captain Selini had refused her location request. How could she possibly proceed with her wedding-planning duties if the location wasn't approved? Given the princess's eagerness to marry, Ava was already working on a short timeline. The captain's refusal was a setback she couldn't afford. She wanted to scream in frustration.

Instead Ava pulled her keys from her purse and pointed the key fob at her car parked in the distance on the opposite side of the cobbled street. Clicking the button on the key fob, she watched with satisfaction as her headlights blinked, signaling that she'd successfully unlocked the car doors.

Good. Nothing more stood between her and her escape route.

"Ms. Wright, please come back."

It was the "please" that made her pause, almost against her will, halfway across the empty street, still a couple hundred feet from her car. She wavered there, undecided, for a few long seconds.

"Please," he repeated, sounding almost pleading.

The pleading note in his voice prompted her to turn back, if only to see the expression on his face. Captain Jason Selini begging? She wouldn't miss it, not after all the trouble he'd given her over the course of the recent royal weddings.

But when she turned to face him, she found he'd stopped in his tracks still dozens of feet from her and his face had gone nearly white.

"Get down!" he shouted, his words buried by an enormous boom behind her.

Ava ducked slightly, unsure what was happening. Time seemed to slow for a moment, and yet everything happened so quickly. She felt a sudden heat envelop her, blowing past her with a furious gust of hot wind. At the same time, she felt something sting her near her ankles.

The captain of the guard threw one arm up to shield his face as he ducked and ran toward her, still shouting something, though the blast of heat that had come from behind her swept forward and took his words away. That, or she couldn't hear anything. Her ears began to ring, a distant, tinny sound that further disoriented her.

Jason was at her side in an instant, one hand firmly propping her up by her elbow. "Let's get you out of here. Are you all right? Can you walk?"

Ava wanted to tell him not to be absurd, that of course she could walk, but as she took half a step forward in an attempt to prove it, the pain at her ankles bit into her furiously.

She looked down at her legs.

Far below her knee-length skirt, blood trickled down her ankles from half a dozen shards of glass that had embedded themselves in her skin.

Ava could only stare at her legs, wondering what had happened. Black smoke billowed toward her and she coughed, turning halfway around to see her car engulfed in flames. "What happened?"

"Car bomb. We've got to get you off the street." The captain's words echoed numbly against her throbbing eardrums.

"My car?" Ava blinked several times, but the smoke and heat stung her eyes, making it difficult to see, and she felt too stunned to think clearly.

"I'll have to carry you," the captain muttered as he bent to inspect the injuries on her legs.

Ava looked at him, horrified at the thought of him carrying her. Determined to prove she was perfectly capable of walking on her own, she tried to take another step forward but wobbled unsteadily, the ringing in her ears messing with her sense of balance. Fortunately she'd been on the far periphery of the blast, and what few shards of glass had flown that far had already fallen low, reaching only to her ankles. Other than the ringing in her ears and the injuries near her Achilles tendons, she didn't think she was hurt.

"I've got to get you off the street in a hurry!" The captain glanced up and down the cobbled path, though Ava saw no further sign of danger, just a bunch of uniformed royal guards pouring out from the pedestrian gate and a car farther up the street pulling out from the curb and driving away.

"What do you mean?" Ava started to ask, but before she'd half spoken the question, the captain had plucked her up with his arms around her waist and tossed her over his shoulder like a bag of potatoes. Her feet stuck out in front in a most undignified manner, and her head bobbed behind him as he trotted quickly back toward the gate to the palace courtyard.

"Sorry. I'll have you down in a minute," he apologized as he ran.

Ava yelped. She wanted to demand to be put down, and yet it had occurred to her that perhaps she didn't want to be on the street, not if cars were going to be exploding. And she wasn't nearly fit to walk, not with the sharp glass digging into her skin with every twitch of her legs and her ringing ears making her feel like a bobblehead doll.

Besides that, there was something oddly thrilling about being carried by the captain of the guard. She couldn't quite put her finger on what it was but attributed it to all the trouble he'd given her and some peculiar sense of justice that he should have to carry her, running and giving orders to his men all at the same time.

In a moment he had her back through the door of the royal-guard headquarters, the building she'd only just left short minutes before. He settled her in a seated position on a hard sofa in the waiting room, with her injured legs sticking stiffly out in front of her. She didn't dare twitch a muscle for fear of being further injured by the glass.

The captain called out to a guard seated behind a bulletproof glass panel, "Oliver, toss me the first-aid kit, will you?"

"Do you need me to assist you?" Oliver asked as he came around by way of a side door and delivered a large cross-emblazoned metal box.

"No. Keep an eye on those security screens and let me know if anything else blows up. And call the Sardis police. Tell them to send over their bomb squad. That car was on their side of the street." As he spoke, Jason Selini gingerly touched Ava's leg, then made a disgusted sound.

"How bad is it?" Ava asked.

"From the looks of it, they're just surface scratches, nothing very deep, but I can take you to the hospital if you'd prefer."

Ava grimaced. She liked to think of herself as a tough, independent woman. She had work to do. Prince Alexander's wedding to Lillian Bardici was to take place in eight days, and she was already in the early stages of planning his little sister Princess Anastasia's wedding, scheduled for just a few months later. Hospital visits were time-consuming, weren't they? "I'm sure it's fine. I can tend to them myself if you need to go out and see to your men."

"You can tend to them yourself?" Jason challenged her, the firm set of his lips bent upward in grim amusement.

Determined to prove her statement, Ava leaned forward, ignoring the pain caused by the movement as her leg muscles stretched.

"Stop that. Now you're making it worse," the captain chided her, snapping on a pair of gloves before tearing open a few small packets.

"What are those?" Ava asked warily. She didn't trust this man, not after the way they'd been arguing mere minutes before. In her mind, Jason Selini was nothing more than an obstacle to her goals. He'd never helped her before.

"Just a little antiseptic." He bent over the cuts on her legs and gingerly plucked out the glass. Finally he looked satisfied with his work. "I believe I got all of the glass out. Once I clean off the blood, I can see what else is there. You're fortunate you weren't any closer to your car—these bits didn't have the full force of the blast behind them. Any closer and you could have been seriously hurt. There." He daubed a bit more with the antiseptic-soaked gauze. "It really wasn't bad at all—just a bit of blood that made everything look worse."

"You're sure you don't need to be outside with your men?"

The captain dug into a package of bandages. "They know what to do. They'll secure the area and then hand things over to the bomb squad as soon as they arrive."

"So this sort of thing happens all the time?" Ava had been in the tiny Mediterranean kingdom of Lydia for ten months—long enough to plan two royal weddings, a handful of titling ceremonies and a royal marriage-renewal ceremony. In that time, she'd heard rumors of violence and danger, and once had her reception hall locked down because of gunmen on the loose within the walls of the palace grounds. But this was the first car bomb she'd ever heard about.

"We haven't had a vehicle explode since the royal motorcade was ambushed last June—almost a year ago now. But those were grenade hits, not bombs."

"Ow!" Ava shrieked before he was quite finished. "Could you be more careful?"

"Sorry. That little piece of glass was hiding."

"Are you sure I don't need stitches?"

Jason held up his gloved hand in front of her, a slender shard of glass perched on one finger. "That's all it was. I'm almost done. There's nothing that needs stitching."

Feeling slightly embarrassed that she'd shrieked for such a tiny piece of glass, Ava mustered up her pride. "I think you're taking far too much satisfaction at seeing my pain, after all the trouble I've caused you," she accused him.

Jason sighed and pasted another adhesive bandage above her ankle. "So you admit you've caused me plenty of trouble."

"No more than you've caused me." She bit her lip as the captain applied more antiseptic, dabbing roughly at her injuries. "You know, you could try to be gentle."

The captain was silent for a moment, but his movements became more precise, with less pressure.

"You know," Jason echoed her as he stuck another bandage carefully in place, "you could thank me."

"For what? You threw me on this couch like you were tossing a sack of kittens in the river."

She expected Jason's sharp retort but instead heard snickering from the doorway, and looked up in time to see a group of royal guards filing back into the building.

"Report," Jason commanded, not sounding the least bit amused.

The men sobered. "All's clear. The Sardis Police Bomb Squad has taken over the crime scene. They've got their bomb-sniffing dogs working the entire perimeter of the palace grounds, three blocks deep. If there's another bomb in the area, they'll find it."

"Good work, men. Back to your stations."

The men filed out in silence, but before the door closed behind them, a voice carried clearly from the hallway. "He would like to toss her in the river like a sack of kittens."

A chorus of guffaws agreed with the statement.

"You didn't hear that," Jason stated bluntly as he spread antiseptic on the last of her cuts.

"Yes, I did," Ava informed him. "And I felt the sting."

The captain applied the last bandage, but that hadn't been the sting she was referring to. Did Jason Selini really want to be rid of her that badly that he'd toss her off a bridge? The captain seemed to be a man of integrity and perfectly upright character, but she knew his resentment toward her ran deep. They'd been in opposition since the very first ceremony she'd planned at the end of the previous summer. She'd ignored his attitude all these long months, just as she habitually ignored anyone who didn't like her. Hadn't she learned her lesson long before? She couldn't please everyone. Best to focus on doing her job and giving her brides the weddings of their dreams. That much she could do.

But the image of her burning car had seared itself into her mind. Why had her car exploded? Had someone placed a bomb inside to hurt her? What if they'd killed her?

"It's all right. I'm done." The captain handed her a tissue.

Only then did Ava realize she'd started sniffling, her

near brush with death somehow penetrating her usually impervious armor. "Why do you think my car blew up?" It took all of her resolve to keep her voice steady.

"Somebody put a bomb in it. From what I saw, they probably had it set to go off a certain number of seconds after you unlocked your door—the idea being that you'd be very near or inside the car at that moment. If you hadn't stopped and turned around, that's where you would have been."

"But—that would have killed me." Ava couldn't get the image of her charred car from her mind—nor could she quite grapple with the idea of what would have become of her if she'd been inside.

The captain met her eyes for just a moment. Instead of hardened anger in his flint-gray eyes, she saw a hint of sympathy, maybe even apology.

The change shook her as much as the realization that she'd narrowly escaped a horrific end. "They wanted me dead?"

The captain closed the box of bandages and tucked them away in the first-aid kit, not meeting her eyes. "That's the only reason I can think of for what I saw."

"But why?"

Jason looked her full in the face, a bit of sadness shimmering in his steel-gray eyes. "Do you have any enemies?"

Ava stared at him for long seconds, her stunned mind taking longer than usual to process her thoughts. Finally she answered, "You."

The captain turned away and began plucking up the bandage wrappers he'd left lying about. "I'm the worst enemy you have?"

She nodded, no longer trusting her voice.

"Then I don't know why anyone would put a bomb in

your car." He sucked in a sharp breath and met her eyes again. "But I intend to find out."

His words hit her with such cold force he might as well have tossed her in an icy river. His statement was part vow, part threat. What would it take to find out who'd tried to kill her? Discussing past relationships? Analyzing all the hurts she'd put behind her, including the ones that had made her who she was? She tried to return the captain's determined gaze, but she found she couldn't keep her head up, not at the prospect of rooting through the skeletons in her closet. That wasn't a place she wished to explore, certainly not with this man who hated her.

But what other choice did she have?

TWO

Jason Selini felt the tiniest glimmer of sympathy toward this woman who'd caused him so many headaches over the past several months. Ava Wright was impossibly stubborn, sharp-tongued and utterly unreasonable once she'd made up her mind to have her way.

And she always got her way. Jason had never been able to override her wishes except for a few times when he'd been able to prove her plans would cause imminent danger to royal life and property. The rest of the time she was a steamroller, exerting her will in spite of all his efforts to make her see reason.

And yet, as he glanced at her now, perched on the edge of the hard sofa in the waiting room of the royal-guard headquarters, she looked shaken. More than that, she looked like a scared little girl, and for the first time he realized she was almost certainly younger than his thirty-three years, in spite of her international success as a wedding planner.

Though the woman usually looked as impeccable as the weddings she planned, the incident had marred her facade. Her hair, which was dyed a harsh red and usually styled in jagged spikes shooting out from her head, now looked as limp and dazed as the rest of her. And her makeup, which had always been flawless, if a bit fierce, was now smeared, making her look eerily like a home-less street urchin, save for the expensive suit and shoes.

With the last of the first-aid items tucked safely away in the case, Jason realized he could delay the inevitable conversation no longer. "I'd like you to come to my office."

"Why?" She blinked up at him, dark smudges outlining her eyes, highlighting the fear that glimmered above the green of her irises.

"I need to get your statement about what happened while everything is still fresh in your memory." He didn't add that he wanted to grill her on possible attackers and motives. Though the crime had technically occurred on the Sardis police side of the street, given the proximity to the palace and Jason's duty to protect the royal family, Jason considered it his job to root out the reasons behind the attack—and prevent anything similar from happening again. He appreciated the expert help of the Sardis bomb squad, and he'd be sure to keep them in the loop with everything he learned, but he wasn't about to sit back and wait for them to do his job for him.

Ava scowled. "You think that's a moment I'm likely to soon forget?"

"Or suppress. It happens all the time. The more violent the incident, the bigger the wall the victim puts up." He extended his hand as a gentlemanly gesture, fully expecting her to refuse it.

To his surprise, she placed her palm in his and leaned against him as she levered herself up from the sofa. It occurred to him that, prior to throwing her over his shoulder moments before, he'd never touched the woman. Her hand felt small and shaky as she held tight to him. From what he knew of her, he was certain she wouldn't have leaned on him at all unless she'd had no other choice. Ava was too independent for that. Her first steps were cautious, but then she walked beside him with increased confidence.

"Your legs okay?"

"Better now, thank you."

Surprised at her thanks, Jason almost smiled. "You're welcome."

He led her back through to his office, where her plans for Princess Anastasia's wedding to Kirk Covington still lay atop his desk. Her requested location was fraught with hazards, even under the best circumstances. Given the explosion that could have killed them both, the plan was all the more unthinkable. He helped her into a chair, then shoved the stapled pages to the side of his desk.

Jason opened up a fresh incident-report template on his computer. "Now, tell me your version of what happened."

Ava sat up straight, looking less shaken already. "We were in here, discussing the plans for Princess Anastasia's wedding location."

Jason did his best to accurately type her words, though he very nearly switched out *discussing* for *arguing about* but caught himself before he hit the wrong keys. The way his screen was angled, Ava might be able to see his words. Best not to upset her further—he knew how obstinate she could be when angered.

"And then?" he prompted once he'd entered all she'd said.

"Well—" she looked at him bluntly "—you were being completely unreasonable—"

"That's not relevant—"

"It's an island." Ava rose on her seat and picked up her previous argument right where she'd left off before stalking out in a huff earlier. "If anything, it's more se-cure than the Sardis Cathedral and just as safe as any-thing within the palace walls."

"The palace complex is the most secure location in Sardis." Jason would have directed Ava back to her statement, but the security of the palace complex wasn't something he could let come under question. Along with ensuring the safety of the members of the royal family, his primary duty was to keep the palace grounds secure at all times.

"Oh!" Ava threw back her head with a sarcastic fake laugh. "And the gunmen who ran amok during Duch-ess Julia's titling ceremony—was that an example—"

Jason gave up trying to type and instead reached across his desk toward the woman, pointing one finger as he spoke. "That is precisely why I can't allow you to attempt to hold a royal wedding on an island. If gun-men can get inside these walls, they can easily attack an island."

"Precisely my point. If either location is equally vul-nerable—"

"They're not vulnerable!" Jason snapped, wishing to end the conversation and get back to typing his report.

"Then there shouldn't be a problem with using the island of Dorsi—"

"The island of Dorsi is off-limits. No one is allowed to step foot on that island."

"All the more reason why it's perfectly—" Ava rose to her feet as she tried to cut off his words.

But Jason would not be interrupted. "It's too danger-ous. It's forbidden!" Jason found he had to stand as well, just to make himself heard. Besides, he couldn't let the redhead tower over him.

"It's absolutely not dangerous. My clients have already vetted the location—"

Outraged, Jason leaned across his desk. "No one is allowed to step foot on Dorsi."

Ava planted her hands on the desktop and glared at him across the shiny surface. "I already have."

"That's impossible."

"Princess Stasi and Kirk Covington took me there to show me where they wanted to hold the ceremony—in the ruins of the ancient cathedral where the Lydian kings and queens of old were married."

"You've been to the island of Dorsi?" Jason had been there once, too—a memory he'd prefer to forget. "It's too dangerous."

"Maybe too dangerous for you."

"I've been there—to retrieve a dead body."

To his satisfaction, Ava looked the slightest bit startled by his words. "Whose dead body?"

"My predecessor, Viktor Bosch. He was captain of the royal guard before me. I was appointed after his death." To Jason's relief, his words silenced the wedding planner. "His death was a direct result of the dangers of the island. I cannot allow—"

But the woman's fury rose with renewed vigor. "You cannot refuse a member of the royal family." She leaned farther across the desk, invading his side.

"I can if it endangers safety." Jason leaned forward again, wishing to push the woman back out of his space, using physical force if necessary. "And I already have." He grabbed a self-inking stamp from his desk drawer and slapped the word against the paper with so much force droplets of red ink splattered around the letters.

Rejected.

Ava grabbed the stack of paper away from him. "You can't—"

Jason tugged back on his half of the papers. He needed to file it with the king's office to make it official. "I already did."

"It's not your decision to make!" Ava tugged on the pages.

Jason felt her fingers slipping and pulled harder, certain he'd nearly gained the advantage. "I've made the decision! It's done," he shouted over her words, even as she increased the volume of her demands.

Suddenly the door across from him swung open, and Jason looked up to see Galen and Titus, two of his royal guardsmen, standing in the open doorway, watching his wrestling match with the wedding planner in obvious shock and amusement.

"We did knock." Titus cleared his throat. "No one answered."

"We heard sounds of distress and felt it in the best interest of your safety to open the door," Galen added.

Hoping to take advantage of the momentary distraction, Jason gave the papers a final hard tug. To his surprise, however, Ava held on so tightly his efforts pulled her partway onto his desk.

The wedding planner glared up at him furiously.

Jason stopped tugging on the papers but didn't release them. While letting her keep hold of the papers wouldn't result in her getting her way, he couldn't bear the thought of giving her the satisfaction of prevailing over him, not when she'd already gotten her way so many times. It was almost as though she held more authority than he did—it hadn't escaped his noticed that his men in the gatehouse had unlocked the pedestrian gate for her, even though he'd been right behind her.

As the youngest captain in the history of the royal guard, he didn't always feel as though his men thought he deserved his position of authority over them. Ava's constant triumphs degraded his power—which complicated his efforts to keep the royal family safe.

Titus continued, "The Sardis bomb squad has found something they want you to see."

Immediately concerned, Jason asked, "Is it safe?"

"It's a small bit of residue on the ground," Galen clarified. "They think it might be bomb-related material. The dogs sniffed it out."

"I'll take a look." Jason glanced at Ava. "You can stay here."

"I'm coming, too." She shot him a look that said she wasn't about to back down.

Having fought the woman enough times before, Jason had learned to pick his battles. He didn't need his men to watch him be defeated by the wedding planner. "Fine. But the papers stay here. And you'll do as I say."

He heard Ava make a noise in her throat, followed by hushed snickers from his men.

Jason chafed, not just that the woman so openly defied him, but that her disobedience was obvious to his men—and apparently amused them to the point of barely stifled disrespect. His men—the royal guards who'd served alongside him for years—were drilled in decorum. They understood ceremony and symbolism and the dignity of their positions. But the newest recruits from the army, including Titus, were a rougher sort, more interested in proving their strength than polishing their shoes. If the royal guard hadn't desperately needed the manpower, he'd have sent the men back to the army.

His inability to control the wedding planner set a particularly bad example for his men. At a time when he wanted the new recruits to learn etiquette and protocol, Ava Wright made them snicker and crack jokes behind his back.

He needed to regain full control of the royal guard.

Too bad the wedding planner seemed equally determined to control everything within her reach.

If he was going to control the royal guard, he'd have to set things straight with the wedding planner first.

Ava watched as the captain bent to inspect what appeared to be a random patch of cobblestones. They were a little over a block away from the place where her car still smoldered, a blackened testimony to the violence that had invaded her morning.

"We've taken samples," a member of the bomb squad told the captain soberly. "We'll have to process them at the lab to learn exactly what it is, but based on the dogs' reaction, it's most likely residue from an explosive."

They stood about eight feet from the sidewalk—where the driver would have stepped through the door of a compact car, had a vehicle still been parked there. Ava tried to sort out what the men were saying. "So whoever put the bomb in my car may have parked here, in this spot?"

"Exactly." Jason nodded. "We can review the footage from the security cameras on the palace wall to see if they picked up anything, although I'll warn you, the cameras are designed to protect the walls, not the streets of Sardis outside our jurisdiction. We might not have gotten much. What was the time window that your car was parked on this street?"

"I arrived to meet with the princess shortly before eight, then stopped by your office to get your approval on the wedding plans. You kept me waiting."

Jason didn't apologize. "The explosion happened

shortly after ten. That's more than a two-hour window. Any number of vehicles may have come and gone in that time."

Though she was tempted to point out to the captain that he might have narrowed the window by agreeing to see her when she'd first arrived at headquarters, another thought made her heart beat with apprehension. "A car pulled away from this spot right after the explosion."

Both the captain and the members of the bomb squad looked surprised.

"You mean you saw a car drive off?" Jason clarified.

Ava nodded, the memory rushing back clearly now. She was certain of what she'd seen. Everything had happened so quickly, and yet she distinctly recalled seeing a car pull away—in the back of her dazed mind, she'd thought to herself the driver was fortunate to have parked ahead of her on the street. Otherwise the vehicle would have had to drive past her smoldering car to leave.

The bomb tech scowled at the captain. "The person witnessed an explosion, but instead of checking to see if everyone was all right, he fled?"

"Maybe he was scared?" Ava suggested, her voice betraying that same emotion.

"Or guilty." Jason ran a frustrated hand through his hair, exposing the silvery flecks that framed his close-cropped ebony hair. "We need to look at that footage. Can you describe the car you saw?"

"It was a car," Ava told him, recalling all she could.

"Make or model?"

Ava bit her lip. She hadn't looked closely enough to see any details—most of her attention had been on the pain in her legs and all the confusion around her. The ringing in her ears hadn't helped her focus at all, either.

"Color?" Jason prompted.

Ava pinched her eyes shut, replaying the memory. "Dark?" She couldn't say anything more certain than that.

To his credit, Captain Selini neither laughed nor rolled his eyes. "We'll have to look at the footage. Are we done here?" he asked the bomb tech.

The squad member nodded. "We'll give you a call when we get the results on those samples."

Ava walked alongside the captain as he headed back toward the pedestrian gate in the palace wall, to the royal-guard headquarters building that lay inside the palace grounds. They passed the smoldering remains of her car, and she glanced at it, her steps wavering as she considered what might have happened if she hadn't stopped and turned back to face the captain.

She could have been killed. At the very least, it would have been her face that was disfigured, instead of her ankles.

Suddenly the captain took hold of her arm. "Are you okay?"

Ava wanted to dismiss his question with a laugh, but she had to struggle to catch her breath, and she felt uncharacteristically unsteady on her feet. Attempting to straighten, to pull away from the support of his hand on her arm, she instead stumbled forward unsteadily, her high heels catching in the gaps between the cobblestones.

Jason clasped one hand around her waist. For an instant, she feared he was going to hoist her over his shoulder and trundle her off as before, but instead he met her eyes with surprising concern. "Don't look at the car," he told her in a soothing voice. "Just walk slowly. One foot in front of the other."

In any other situation, Ava would have snapped at him. But it was all she could do to lean on his arm and step slowly forward as instructed. She glanced at his face and found his eyes on hers, concerned, reassuring. His eyes, which had only ever seemed cold and steel-gray before, now held a hint of compassion she hadn't expected.

"I am not an invalid," she told him sharply as soon as she found her voice. She needed to push him away. It was her personal policy not to trust anyone. She'd learned that lesson the hard way, enough that she didn't usually forget. Trust led to pain. Always.

And yet, for the moment at least, it seemed she needed him. His strong arm kept her upright, when otherwise she might fall. She felt so light-headed, the memory and the fear swirling together in her mind. What would have happened if Jason hadn't stopped her from reaching her car? And why had someone planted a bomb there? Granted, she didn't go out of her way to be nice to people—not anymore, not since the two people she most trusted on earth had taken advantage of her trust so horribly.

But surely her newfound assertiveness hadn't prompted the attack. Perhaps she had become prickly, maybe even harsh. She'd only meant to keep people from getting too close to her. She'd never dreamed it would be enough to provoke someone to attempt to kill her.

THREE

Jason watched the images on the security screens as Oliver replayed the relevant moments. As he'd feared, Ava's car had been parked on the edge of the security camera's range, with only the rear bumper in view. The vehicle she'd watched drive away moments after the explosion had been far beyond that. They didn't get so much as a shadow.

"That's it?" Ava asked impatiently from where she stood near his elbow. "You haven't got a single image of any of it?"

"You parked beyond the range of our cameras," Jason explained, trying to keep the frustration he felt from entering his voice. The woman could be difficult to deal with on a good day. She was already upset enough.

"I normally park closer, but that was the nearest spot when I arrived this morning."

Convinced the screens had nothing more to show him, Jason turned to face the wedding planner. Her tone might have been icy, but her eyes were round with fear.

As well they should be. Among the many questions that vied for his attention, the foremost was whether the woman had been specifically targeted, or if her car had been randomly chosen for its position near the palace, but beyond the range of his cameras. Until he could answer with confidence that she had no more to fear than anyone else, he needed to take steps to keep her safe.

"Stay here and review the footage," he told her. "I have some phone calls to make."

Jason strode to his office, thinking quickly. There were apartments built into the rear wall of the palace grounds. Once used to house servants of the royal family, they continued to provide lodging for long-term guests and staff, even some of his guards. If he could secure a vacancy, the wedding planner could stay inside the safety of the palace walls, under the watchful eyes of his guards.

"Where are you going?" Ava's demanding tone carried down the hall after him.

Jason mustered up his patience as he called back to her, "To my office to make some phone calls."

"So you're just leaving me? That's it? I don't have a car anymore. What am I supposed—"

He raised a hand to shush her. "The phone calls are for your benefit. I'm trying to find you a place to stay."

"It was my car that blew up, not my apartment."

"You don't need a car." Jason reached his office and hurried inside, wishing he could close the door and keep her out.

"Yes, I do! I have a business to run." She stomped into the office after him. "I've got a wedding in eight days and another in less than four months. I have work to do."

"The guards can drive you."

"Guards? I don't want—"

"I don't care what you want. It's for your safety. I'm going to find you a place to stay near the guards."

"I don't want to stay near your guards! They want to

throw me in the river like a sack of kittens." A note of despair carried through her bossy tone.

"No, that was me, as I recall." Jason hoped his admission might deflate her anger. For a moment, as he glanced at her to gauge the effect of his words, he thought he caught a glimmer of gratitude in her eyes—as though she understood the effort he'd put into his gracious words and appreciated the gesture.

But in an instant, cold fury snapped into her eyes again. "You wish I'd made it to my car before the bomb went off, don't you?"

Jason glared at her, wondering if he'd imagined the gratitude in her eyes. Why would she be so mean to him if she understood he was trying to assuage her concerns? He'd wondered before, while arguing with her, if she wasn't actually trying to pick a fight with him, to egg him on instead of making peace.

But why would she do that?

Really, for all he'd done for her that morning, bandaging her cuts and dropping everything else on his morning schedule, she ought to have shown him a little appreciation. "I wish the bomb hadn't gone off at all. I wish there'd been no bomb. But since there was, and since you were the recipient, intended or not, we've got to put you under guard."

"I don't see why."

"Someone may be trying to kill you. That car that pulled away may have been the bomber, waiting to see if his efforts worked. If so, he knows you're still alive. Given the risks he's taken so far, there's no reason to think he isn't going to try again."

Ava blinked at him. "I don't have time for this. I have work to do."

"So do I. The longer I argue with you, the further I

fall behind. Let me make some phone calls and we'll see what we can do to keep you safe until we sort this out."

Theresa Covington, the palace household manager, answered his phone call. He inquired about an available room among the palace-wall apartments and was relieved that Theresa was able to reserve an apartment for Ava. "Thank you, Theresa. Have a lovely day." He closed the call with the household manager and smiled at Ava.

She scowled at him. "What?"

"I'll drive you to your apartment so you can pack a bag."

"I'm not staying among your guards."

"You'll have your own apartment. There are guards also staying in the palace-wall apartments. Theresa told me you stayed in one when you first arrived in Lydia, before you found your own place." Jason stepped past her down the hall, poking his head into the switchboard room to tell Oliver where he was going.

Ava followed him, still frowning. "I don't appreciate this loss of my freedom. I have an important job to do."

In spite of her protests, she followed him to the royal garages.

Jason chose a bulletproof vehicle. Only the new limousines, ordered since the insurgent ambush the previous summer, had armor plating, and he couldn't justify driving the wedding planner in a limo. The bulletproof sedan should be more than adequate for a quick trip to Ava's apartment.

Fortunately Ava's place wasn't far from the palace complex, and the drive passed in silence. Jason would have fumed at the woman's rudeness, except that he'd seen that glimmer of fear in her eyes, that wounded little girl who'd peeked out when she thought no one was looking, and he began to wonder if she wasn't picking fights with him on purpose. Perhaps her anger was a ruse to distract him from something deeper. But what?

Jason parked in front of Ava's building, just across the street from her door. "Wait for me to walk you in," he told her as he put the car in Park and turned off the engine.

But to his chagrin, the woman ignored him, stepping out as he pulled the keys from the ignition and opened the driver's side door. Ava quickly rounded the front of the vehicle and glanced up and down the empty street before darting across toward her door.

Jason saw it all in a single glance—Ava's unsteady, injured trot across the two empty traffic lanes; the charcoal-gray Volkswagen Jetta that pulled out from the curb just over a block away the moment Ava turned her attention from looking both ways to walking; and the squeal of tires that betrayed the VW's sudden acceleration.

Jason leaped into action, shouting at Ava to hurry as he ran toward her. She was already in progress crossing the street. The car approached in the same lane he'd been driving in, on the side of the street opposite her apartment. If she hurried, she'd be out of the way in time.

But even as Jason bounded toward her, he glimpsed the car swerving toward them, into the other lane. Ava was hobbling far too slowly in her three-inch heels. She'd never make it.

With only half a second to act, Jason scooped an arm around Ava's waist and leaped with her toward the curb. He had her nearly to the sidewalk when the Jetta, oblivious of the curb or the neat little flower patch in front of Ava's apartment, swerved onto the sidewalk, knocking his legs out from under him and sending his back smashing into the windshield and side mirror.

It was a glancing blow, but the force was enough to

send them both airborne for several feet. Jason tightened his arms around Ava, tucking her head into the relative safety of his chest as they hit the sidewalk and rolled.

He looked for the car, fearful the vehicle might swing around and take a second pass. The two of them were high up on the sidewalk now, nearly against the steps of Ava's building, but the curb hadn't stopped the car before, and if it decided to pin them to the concrete steps, not even his embrace would shield the wedding planner from injury.

To his relief, he saw the Jetta disappear over the rim of the hill, speeding away. Unfortunately, given the distance, he couldn't make out the plate number.

Jason turned his attention to Ava next. "Are you okay?" He had her still tucked tight against him, but pulled back just far enough so he could see her face.

One red-nailed hand clutched his shirt. She blinked up at him. "What was that?"

Even more disheveled than after her last brush with death, the wedding planner didn't look at all her usual prickly, put-together self. Jason felt his heart twist with sympathy. "That," he groaned as he rolled onto his back in preparation for sitting up, "is proof that whoever bombed your car this morning is targeting you specifically."

Ava pinched her eyes shut and held tight to Captain Selini's shirt. She didn't like the man—couldn't stand him most days—but right now she'd have gladly buried her face against his shoulder and sobbed.

The captain spoke rapidly into his earpiece, instructing his dispatcher to send men in a car. But his words came in shallow gasps and his face turned deep red as he struggled to breathe.

"Are you okay?" Ava asked in a whisper, scrutinizing his features as she awaited his response. Had the car simply knocked the wind from his lungs, or was he seriously injured?

Her conscience stabbed her. If she'd waited to cross the street with him as he'd said, would they still have been hit? The car had struck him directly and thrown him hard against the cement. What if he died because she hadn't listened?

It occurred to Ava as she stared at his face that the captain wasn't as old as she'd assumed him to be, in spite of the early gray that flecked his hair. For all the times she'd argued with him, she'd never bothered to look at him closely—part of her personal policy against getting close to any person in any way. But now as she watched him from inches away, she realized he was hardly any older than she was.

Jason Selini groaned as he sucked in a breath.

Ava rolled onto her side, out of his way as he struggled to sit up. "Can I help you?" she asked, extending one hand, realizing only when she saw that her hands were empty that she'd left the plans for Princess Anastasia's wedding in the car. Suddenly the plans didn't seem so important. The captain appeared to be in real pain.

"Is your back broken?"

Jason winced. "I'm wearing body armor." He strained to breathe. "That took the bulk of the blow, probably saved us both, but my steel plate is dented now." Captain Selini grasped the steps as he pulled himself to standing. "Let's get off this street."

Suddenly fearful that the dark car might return, Ava hurried to her door and let them into the small shared foyer, then led the way to her apartment door, unlocking it carefully.

"Wait." Jason's hand covered hers. "They know where you live. They were waiting for us." He ran his hands around the door frame. Ava assumed he was checking for trip wires or a triggering device of some nature.

Fear pounded from Ava's heart to her ears in one beat. "They'd have to come through the front door to get to this one. They're both locked."

"Open it slowly." The captain relented, straining to breathe, his face frightfully red.

Wishing she could hurry and help the captain before he passed out, Ava nonetheless did as instructed, watching and waiting, ready to spring away if the captain gave any sort of signal at all.

But nothing happened. Her apartment looked the same way it always did—blank white walls, minimal decor, honey-oak wooden floor gleaming in the midday sunlight.

Captain Selini clutched his chest as he stepped inside, talking into his earpiece, between gasping breaths reporting on what had happened.

"Are you sure you're all right?" Ava closed the door behind him, then peered up into his face as he bent over, his face more purple than red.

"My armor." The captain twisted to one side, grimaced and turned back again, panting. "It's cutting into my diaphragm."

"Do you need to take it off?"

"Can you help me?"

Ava wasn't sure what to do, but she figured the captain must be in terrible pain to ask her to help him. Quickly, she unbuttoned the front of his uniform. Purple-faced and fumbling, he explained to her the straps and fasteners, and she pulled him free of the steel-plated body armor.

He straightened immediately, his white T-shirt moving against his well-muscled back and shoulders as he pulled in a real breath for the first time since the car had struck, and flexed his brawny arms backward, testing his range of motion slowly.

For a moment, all Ava could do was stare. She'd always assumed the captain, like all the other guards, was strong. They had physical-fitness requirements for their job, no doubt, so of course they worked out. But she wasn't at all aware of how very physically fit the captain was until he threw his beefy arms up over his head and flexed his muscles, pulling in a deep breath as he assured himself of his full mobility.

Ava's mouth went dry and she watched him in silence. No, he wasn't as old as she'd assumed. The man appeared to be youthful and fit and actually almost attractive, now that she paid attention. Of course, he had that permanent frown line between his eyebrows that made him seem older. But other than the ever-present scowl on his face, Captain Selini was...handsome.

Rather than gawk, Ava returned to the tiny kitchenette that adjoined her open living space. "Can I get you something to drink, or an ice pack? What can I do?"

"Get packed before that guy returns."

"Was he a guy?" Ava asked as she stepped from the kitchenette to the bedroom to gather her things.

"I don't know. The glare of sunlight on the windshield made it difficult for me to see him, but I thought the driver looked male. Did you get a look at him?"

"I barely saw the car at all," Ava confessed. She pulled out her duffel bag, then stared at her open closet and tried to think. How long was she planning to be gone? What should she pack? And what if the man who'd tried twice now to kill her showed up again? Perhaps she ought to choose more practical footwear. She only had eight days until Prince Alexander's wedding. The adventures of the morning had already disrupted her schedule.

She gulped a breath, trying to clear her head, to focus on what she needed to pack and not think any more about what it had felt like to be in Captain Selini's arms. He had such very nice arms. And his manly scent was alluring, as well. That was another thing for her not to think about.

"What can I do to help?"

Ava spun around to find the captain standing in her doorway, looking very uncaptain-like in his T-shirt. Instead he looked like any normal person, but with extra-strong arms that had wrapped around her and saved her from the car. The terror she'd felt in that moment tore through her again, and she shuddered to think how close they'd both come to horrific injury, or worse. "Are you sure you're all right?"

"I never said I was."

"Can I get you an ice pack, then?"

"You can get packed so we can get out." The captain stepped into the small room, making it feel that much tinier with his wide shoulders occupying so much of the space.

"How long do I need to pack for?"

"A couple days should be fine. We can send a team back later to get the rest. Just grab the necessities, or I'll do it for you. We need to get you to safety as soon as possible. I need to figure out what's going on."

Rather than let the captain make good on his threat to select her wardrobe choices for her, Ava tossed clothes into the bag. "What do you think is going on?" she asked as she darted toward her bathroom for everything else she'd need.

"Somebody's trying to kill you." The captain's tone

was so grim Ava couldn't help looking up as she stepped past him, then froze as his gray eyes locked on hers.

"Kill me?" she repeated. On some level, she'd realized as much already, but hearing him speak the words so bluntly made it all seem real in a way she wasn't ready to deal with yet.

"Given the two attempts so close together, I'd say they're in a hurry about it."

Ava felt her arms go limp as her duffel bag sagged toward the floor. Why would someone want to kill her? What was she supposed to do? Would they strike again at any moment? Overwhelmed, Ava hung her head.

"Hey." Captain Selini's hand fell gently on her shoulder, a tiny gesture of comfort in the midst of the cold fear that gripped her. His strong hand sent an unwelcome tingle of awareness through her. Normally she'd have shaken him off, but his touch imparted comfort. And she desperately needed comfort, no matter how much she resented that fact.

She looked up into his face, still surprised to see how handsome he looked at close range, when he wasn't yelling at her, when she actually looked at him long enough to see past the silver flecks, which she realized now were probably brought on by the stress of his job or possibly as a result of arguing so many times with her. If it hadn't been for her personal policy never to get close to anyone, she might have given in to the impulse to lean toward him, to bury her face against his strong shoulder and sob.

But instead of inviting her to lean against him and cry, the captain gave her a tiny shake. "Get going. We need to leave in two minutes. Pull yourself together."

FOUR

Jason turned and left Ava alone to pack her bag. He needed to breathe—preferably in a room that didn't smell floral and feminine. Still unsure how badly he'd been injured, he pulled his arms back and flexed his muscles again. Sore. Very, very sore. But nothing froze up or refused to move. Nothing felt broken.

He examined what he could of the sparse apartment, searching for clues that might explain why someone would want to kill the wedding coordinator. An event gone bad, perhaps? Surely any offended party would sue before resorting to murder. Jason scoured the room and noticed a desktop with a smattering of documents littering the surface.

Postcards of the kingdom of Lydia—unaddressed, unsent. Ava must have bought them to share with friends back home in the United States. Brochures of various florists, musicians…nothing he wouldn't have expected a wedding planner to have on her desk. But perhaps she'd offended one of the vendors represented on the brochures. Would an angry dressmaker resort to murder? Jason scooped up the brochures. They were worth looking into.

As he shuffled the glossy pages into his hands, Jason

found something different—a photograph, fairly large but unframed, a close-up of a woman's face. It was by far the most personal item Jason had seen on the desk. He stopped shuffling pages long enough to look at the woman. She was pretty, her brown hair in loose curls tumbling around her face, her eyes twinkling, her full lips spread in a broad, happy smile.

"I need everything from that desk, too."

Jason turned to see Ava standing in the doorway, her duffel slung over her shoulder. He realized the woman in the picture looked a lot like Ava. A sister, perhaps? Ava stepped toward him, a second bag gaping wide. She held it out, and he dropped the brochures with the picture on top of the other items into the bag.

Ava gave a little yelp, reached for the picture, then shook her head quickly and closed the bag instead.

At the same moment Jason heard a vehicle outside. He turned to see an bulletproof royal-guard sedan come to a stop double-parked beside the car he'd driven earlier. "Let's go." Jason grabbed his body armor and uniform shirt, but Ava's reaction to the picture didn't sit well with him. "Who's in the picture?"

A horrified expression flashed across the wedding planner's face, followed by reddening cheeks. "Where did you find that?"

"It was on your desk with the brochures." Intrigued by her response and wondering if he was onto something, he prodded further. "Is it your sister?"

"I'm an only child." She pulled the door open and waited for him to step into the foyer.

"It's got to be a relative of some sort." Jason hovered next to her as they opened the outer door. Two guards stepped from the car—Titus and Adrian, two of the recent transfers from the Lydian army. They looked ready for war in their helmets, with automatic rifles—not the usual image he liked his royal guards to project, but given the circumstances, he almost felt relieved by their rough-and-ready approach.

"Why does it matter?" Ava asked as they stepped down the stairs to the sidewalk, where she peered anxiously in both directions.

Jason tried to shrug, but his back protested, so he said simply, "She's pretty." Nodding to his men, he led Ava quickly across the street and into the bulletproof car.

"Well, thank you," Ava said as he opened her door first and took her bag from her shoulder.

Jason raised a questioning eyebrow.

"The picture?" Ava pointed. "It's me." She sat inside the car and pulled the door shut after herself as Jason shook off his surprise and hurried back around to the driver's side. With no sign of the Jetta anywhere, his men got back into their car, ready to follow him back to the palace.

Jason shot Ava a quick, assessing glance as he started the car and pulled carefully away from the curb. Maybe the lovely girl in the picture really was Ava, but that raised even more questions in his mind—such as why any woman who could look so pretty would choose instead to make herself appear so severe. "I've never seen you smile," he realized aloud as he drove back toward the palace, watching his mirrors carefully for any sign of the attack Jetta, grateful for the presence of his men in the car behind them.

"I make it a policy not to," Ava told him bluntly.

"Why not?"

She sighed and settled back against her seat. "It's a long story."

"Is it?" He stepped on the accelerator as he pulled

away from a stoplight. "Well, get ready to tell it. I want to hear all your stories."

"What? You can't be serious."

"Somebody wants to kill you. You're going to help me figure out who it is."

Ava stared at the street ahead and bit her lip. She would not cry. No way was she going to let the maddening captain of the Lydian Royal Guard see her cry.

But at the same time, she felt terrified at the thought of sharing anything about her past. Couldn't the bomb squad analyze the residue they'd found on the street and track down the killer that way? Wasn't that how crimes were solved on television? Why should she have to spill all her painful secrets?

She should have thrown away the engagement photo instead of cutting Dan out of the picture and saving the rest. Why hadn't she? It was a flattering picture of her, true, but it wasn't as though she was going to use the head shot for promotional purposes. She didn't even look like that anymore.

With a guilty swirl in her stomach, Ava realized she hadn't tossed the picture because she'd wanted a reminder of what it had felt like to be happy—not simply because she doubted she'd ever be that happy again, but as a caution should she ever allow herself to trust anyone as much as she'd trusted Dan. Happiness was stupid, a fool's fancy.

That was why she'd kept the picture.

Too soon, they arrived at the palace. Jason parked the car inside the garage. His men who'd followed them parked their car and met him in the expansive cobbled driveway.

"Accompany Ms. Wright to apartment 8-B in the

palace-wall apartments. Theresa Covington was going to send over a housekeeping team to check her in—they should be there by now."

Offended that he was dumping her so abruptly, Ava glared at the captain. "You're not coming with me?"

"I have important things to do."

Ava looked at the guards. She couldn't be sure, but she was nearly certain one of them had cracked the joke about tossing her in the river. And the other one had laughed when he'd said it. She didn't want to be left with these men. Captain Selini might be impossibly stubborn, but she knew she could trust him. He'd saved her life twice that day—once on purpose, even.

She grabbed the captain's arm as he started to walk away. "What am I supposed to do?" she hissed at him, not wanting the other guards to guess she didn't want to be left with them.

"Whatever you usually do." The captain's grin was half challenge. "You're a very busy woman. You've got an important wedding in eight days and another four months after that." He quoted her words back at her, one eyebrow raised as if to dare her to deny his claim.

He'd won—and he knew it. She could tell by the triumphant angle of his smirk.

Ava blew out a frustrated breath. "Come on, you two," she told the guards, readjusting her bag over her shoulder as she marched toward the sidewalk that led to the apartments on the rear palace wall. Her ankles hurt almost as much as her feelings, but she wouldn't let these men see her pain.

She'd learned a long time ago not to let her feelings show. Why should two attempts on her life change anything?

* * *

Jason wasn't really surprised to see Ava appear in his office doorway shortly after lunch. She'd fixed her hair and makeup, donned a zebra-print top and white slacks that covered her ankle injuries. She appeared ready to behave like her usual impossible self.

"Well, that didn't take long," Jason said by way of greeting.

"What?" She narrowed her eyes warily.

"For you to get your tiger stripes back in place." He meant the words as a subtle jab, but the by the way Ava threw her shoulders back, he guessed she took them as a compliment. "To what do I owe this visit?"

"I need to go out."

"My men can drive you. I've assigned Titus and Adrian to take care of you."

Ava glanced down the hall, then stepped into the room and pulled the door closed solidly behind her. "I don't want them following me."

Jason should have guessed she wouldn't want to cooperate—if only because she always had to argue. "You need protection. Someone's trying to kill you."

"And do you really think your men would stop them?" She leaned over his desk as she had so many times before. But this time, instead of yelling, she kept her voice low, almost pleading. "They don't like me. I want you to come with me."

Jason exhaled with exasperation. "I have things to do. I'm the captain of the guard. We've got a royal wedding in just over a week, and a bomb went off outside our gates this morning. I'm busy." He glared at her.

When she glared silently back at him, he added, "I don't like you any more than they do."

"Good." Ava stood straight. "Anyway, everything's

in place for Alexander's wedding. It's Princess Anastasia's timeline that worries me. I should have the venue established by now."

"Sardis Cathedral," Jason volunteered. "The same as every other royal wedding in the history of Lydia."

"Not every royal wedding in the history of Lydia," Ava corrected him sharply. "Before Castlehead was abandoned, the kings and queens were always married—"

"We're not going to Dorsi." Jason stood and crossed his arms over his chest, refusing to wince at the pain in his aching back. "I don't want to hear you speak of it again. It's absolutely beyond question."

"You don't want me to speak of it again?" Ava raised an eyebrow. When Jason nodded, she continued, "I'll make you a deal. I won't ever bring it up again if you'll accompany me to the island and hear the plans I've laid out for Anastasia's wedding."

Jason clenched his teeth, torn. He hated to let the woman have her way, even one tiny bit. However, he had planned to spend the rest of his afternoon—and even his evening, if necessary—grilling her about her past, searching for any hint of who might be trying to kill her. Alexander's wedding was coming up far too soon for them to fire Ava and find someone else, but at the same time, if someone was trying to kill her, the whole palace was in danger. The bomb outside that morning had proved that.

Going to Dorsi would provide him with the necessary time and isolation to talk to Ava freely and ask her every question he could think of. It would also get her out of the city, away from where the attempts on her life had taken place and—should trouble attempt to follow them—far from the royal family he'd vowed to protect.

If it carried the bonus of convincing her to drop the Dorsi request once he'd heard her out, so much the better.

He uncrossed his arms. "Fine. We'll go to Dorsi. How soon can you be ready to leave?"

"I'm ready now."

"Good. You'll have to promise me you'll do whatever I say—the island is dangerous."

Her triumphant glare didn't falter. "As long as you hear me out, I'll do whatever you say."

Ava brought along the duffel bag containing all the brochures and papers from her desktop. She adjusted the strap over her shoulder as she followed the captain down the dock to a royal-guard speedboat. If Captain Selini wanted to ask her about possible suspects, she'd be ready with the brochures. They could analyze any and every vendor she'd ever worked with—as well as those she'd rejected—and root out possible suspects among them. Anything to keep the captain busy and too distracted to ask about her personal life.

There was no reason for Jason Selini to know anything about her past. Everyone she'd ever known or loved or cared about was half a world away, in Seattle, her hometown. The distance was far too great for any of them to be suspects. No, surely some angry cake decorator had gone off the deep end and decided to target her for not fully appreciating his buttercream frosting.

The captain hopped aboard and extended one hand toward Ava. She ignored the proffered help and planted one foot on the boat, determined to prove that, while she might be injured, she was by no means helpless.

As her foot touched the gleaming white step, the boat shifted, bobbing in the water. Ava hadn't anticipated the motion, but, firmly intending to recover her balance on her own, she pushed off the pier with her other foot. The captain had hopped into the boat with grace. She could do so, as well.

The boat, however, wasn't cooperating, and the bulky bag over her shoulder didn't help. She careened forward, swung her arms wide and nearly punched the captain as he reached to steady her.

She landed hard against his shoulder and yelped.

"Steady now?" Jason asked, his hands surprisingly gentle on her arms as he held her upright.

She glanced up into his face, furious when she spotted amusement sparkling in his gray eyes. "I would be fine if—" She tried to think. Surely somehow her blunder was his fault, or could at least be blamed on him.

"If you'd taken my hand when I'd first offered it?" He looked far too pleased with himself.

Ava glared at him and pulled away, perhaps a bit too suddenly. Only Jason's grip still secure on her arms kept her from tumbling backward.

"If this boat didn't rock so much!" she shot back at him.

"Boats do that." He watched her a moment longer, letting go of her arms but standing close, ready to catch her again if she tipped.

"I'm fine," she assured him, flustered that she'd crashed into his shoulder and further distraught that he had such nice shoulders for crashing into. If she was going to embarrass herself, she'd have preferred to do so in front of someone who wasn't so strong and handsome.

"Can I help you to your seat?" Jason offered.

Though she would rather have walked herself, Ava wished to avoid crashing into those shoulders again, so she took hold of his hand this time, though she glared at him the entire way to the seat and especially once she'd sat down. And she didn't say thank-you, because she didn't feel thankful at all. In fact, she quite resented needing his help.

To her relief, the captain ignored her as he got the boat started and pointed them out to sea. Ava watched carefully, still not completely trusting him to take her to the forbidden island of Dorsi.

The Lydian capital city of Sardis sat on the Mediterranean coast, on the tip of the tiny kingdom nestled between Greece and Albania. The island of Dorsi was the most remote of the dozens of islands that formed an archipelago extending out from the mainland. Once a peninsula connected by land to Sardis, the islands had been washed free by centuries of storms.

Dorsi had once been known as Castlehead, but after hurricanes and crumbling shorelines had rendered the former Lydian palace uninhabitable, the royal family had relocated to the palace in Sardis. Because of the island's history and Princess Stasi's own adventures there with her fiancé, Kirk Covington, the affianced pair wanted to be married in the ruins of the palace cathedral.

In Ava's mind, the island was the perfect spot for a private wedding, which was what the youngest princess wanted. And Ava always gave her brides what they wanted—that promise, and her ability to fulfill it, made her one of the top wedding planners in Seattle, before she'd left everything to come to Lydia.

Kirk Covington had warned her of the supposed dangers of the island. Dorsi was said to have been contaminated by land mines during the World Wars, though Ava had never heard explained what enemy had placed them, since Lydia had remained neutral throughout those conflicts. Besides that, the massive blocks of limestone that teetered in ruinous towers were rumored to fall at the slightest provocation, especially when disturbed by those who didn't belong there.

The island itself was such a formidable rock that there didn't seem to be any decent spot to anchor, and if that weren't deterrent enough, the periphery of the island was dotted every twenty feet or so with fearsome signs, warning potential visitors of certain death should they venture there.

But no rocks had fallen when she'd visited the island with Kirk and Stasi. Indeed, the peaceful Mediterranean shores had looked to her like the perfect location for a private wedding, just foreboding enough to keep the paparazzi at a distance. She only had to convince Jason Selini to agree with her. Perhaps if she cooperated with his investigation questions, he'd be more willing to see things her way.

FIVE

Jason wove the boat between islands, choosing an indirect route to Dorsi for a number of reasons. He wanted more time to talk to Ava, not because he cared to be with her a moment longer than necessary, but because he needed answers, and she adeptly avoided providing them.

In addition to that, he felt sobered by the back-to-back attempts on her life. Whoever had tried to kill her that morning clearly wanted the job done quickly. There was every likelihood he'd been watching the palace and even a slim chance the would-be killer might try to follow them out to sea.

By weaving through the islands, Jason would increase his chances of identifying any watercraft that might be following them, or lose such a tail in the process. But every time he glanced behind them, Jason saw only innocent-looking sailboats, speedboats and Jet Skis manned by vacationers and retirees bent only on enjoying the glorious Lydian seashore on the lovely early-summer day.

If anyone was trying to follow them, he was as good at evasive maneuvers as Ava, who kept his every question focused solely on her work contacts, never anything that touched her personal life. Besides making him frustrated, her intentional avoidance raised his curiosity. What was Ava trying to hide, and why was she so determined to hide it?

His suspicions raised, Jason took the long way around a distant island and glared at Ava, meeting her eyes when she tried to look away. "I want to know about you," he told her bluntly, after she'd headed off his less-pointed questions. "Where do you come from? Who do you care about?"

Ava pressed her back against the passenger's chair and glared at him. "I'm from Seattle. I don't care about anyone."

"You don't care about anyone?" He tested her. Cold though the woman might be, he doubted her words could be true. Even the spiky-haired wedding planner had to care for someone, didn't she? "What about friends, family?"

"I don't have any siblings. My mother died last year, and my father and I—we haven't been on speaking terms since."

"So nobody likes you. You've made it a point to keep it that way. Why?"

The wedding planner turned away from him and looked out to sea, blinking rapidly. Perhaps the wind bothered her eyes. It had stirred loose her hair from its frozen dome, causing it to flutter in the misty sea breeze like real hair instead of spiked armor.

Or perhaps she was blinking away tears. Had he hit on something, a tender spot with real feelings underneath? He sensed he'd struck a nerve. Would probing deeper reveal the identity of the murderer who was after her? It was worth a try to find out.

"Why don't you talk to your father anymore?"

"We don't see eye to eye. He's stubborn and demanding."

"Is that where you got it from?" Jason gave her a quick glance before returning his attention to the sea. He knew the islands well from growing up in Sardis and boating along the archipelago often, but this far from the city, the open currents of the sea could shift underwater rock formations overnight. Not only did he have to watch the water, but he also looked behind them to be certain they were alone.

Empty blue water trailed out behind them, his view cut off by the island they'd just rounded. If someone was trying to follow them, he was staying plenty far behind.

"What does my father have to do with the murderer who's after me?" Ava's voice sounded slightly unsteady.

Jason couldn't let her emotional state distract him from pursuing a possible lead. Her life was at stake. "Somebody is trying to kill you," he reminded her bluntly. "Murder isn't the usual response to a professional slight. Whoever wants you dead has to have a good reason—something bigger than having their table toppers rejected."

"Wedding planning is a cutthroat business," Ava told him, though her voice lacked its usual sharp edge. "It's not all flowers and cake."

"I want to know why nobody likes you. Didn't you ever have any friends?"

"No!" Ava snapped back too abruptly, even for her. "No, I never did."

"But your clients all seem to love you. They recommend you to their friends. The royal family adores you." Jason couldn't deny that truth, though he'd never figured out the discrepancy between her prickliness toward him and her devotion to her brides.

"They adore my *work*," Ava corrected him. "They love *the wedding planner*. They don't even know *me*."

Jason glanced around the boat again, but the route to Dorsi sent him swinging west. He was onto something. Ava had issues, that much was certain. He believed her earlier claim that she didn't smile anymore. She'd said it was a deliberate choice and the reason was a long story. What was the story? Would it explain her issues with people and her refusal to smile? Would it provide the clues he needed to understand why someone wanted to kill her?

He had to find out. "How did you come to be a wedding planner?"

Ava let out a long breath. "I don't see what this has to do—"

"You promised you'd answer my questions," Jason reminded her.

"Fine. All right." She drummed her enameled-red fingernails on the side rail as though the discussion made her nervous. "My father is a minister at a very large church in Seattle. There are several ministers at the church, but he's always been the one to do most of the weddings. He'd have one nearly every week, sometimes more than one each week. When I was young I loved going to rehearsals and even the weddings with him. I loved the music and the dresses, the flowers, pageantry, the promise of happiness and—" She stopped short.

Jason suspected she'd been going to say *love*. Before he could wonder at her deliberate omission, she continued.

"Before long, I knew everything there was to know about weddings. I'd tasted all the cakes, heard all the soloists and string quartets. I knew where the spare microphones were and who to call if someone fell sick at the last moment or got stuck on the East Coast in a blizzard. I could talk a nervous bride out of vomiting—that's harder than it sounds. Once they start to hyperventilate, they're almost certain to lose it. You have to watch their eyes. If they roll back, grab a bucket and try to spare the gown."

Jason couldn't help grinning at the image of the strictly business wedding planner swooping in to rescue a bride from her own nerves, especially given the animated way Ava spoke, the way her eyes lit up as she talked about the job she loved. So Ava Wright wasn't entirely heartless. She cared about brides and loved weddings. According to the brochures in her duffel bag, her wedding-planning business in the U.S. had been called Happily Ever After. Yet Ava herself made it a point never to smile, let alone feel happy. Why not?

"So how did you and your father end up not speaking to each other? It sounds to me as though you worked together."

"We worked together just fine for years, though as my business branched out I worked with other churches." Ava nibbled her lower lip before speaking, her voice softer now, so that Jason had to strain to hear over the sound of the boat and the sea. "Last fall my mother was hit by a car while crossing the street in front of our family home. The doctors put her on life support. My father insisted on pulling the plug. I begged him not to. I told him he was killing her, but he did it anyway."

Jason felt a knot form in his throat. So Ava had a heart after all. And it had been hurt. Badly. "I'm sorry."

"It's all in the past. I got a call from Queen Monica the week after my mother's funeral, wanting to know if I could plan the vow-renewal ceremony for her and King Thaddeus. Monica and her sister Julia had been bridesmaids in weddings I'd done in Seattle—they grew up there, you know. She knew me and trusted me. I came to Lydia. They asked me to stay on for the rest of the royal weddings. I returned to Seattle just long enough to pack my essential things and dispose of the rest."

Ava turned to him from looking out to sea. "So you see, I left everyone in Seattle behind months and months ago. No one there has any reason to think about me, much less want to murder me. The threat must be coming from Lydia. Perhaps someone doesn't want Prince Alexander's wedding to go off well. Have you thought of that? Kill the wedding planner, ruin the wedding."

"I thought you said Prince Alexander's wedding was ready to go, save for the final rehearsal."

"Yes, but I do have a number of final meetings next week. And anyway, a murderer wouldn't necessarily know that I've got all the plans made already." Ava blew out an impatient huff. "The threat has to be coming from Lydia. That's all there is to it."

But Jason wasn't ready to accept that fact, not when the survey of Ava's past had revealed so much. Bracing himself for what might be an angry response, he asked a hard question. "Who was driving the car that hit your mother?"

Instead of anger, Ava winced as though she'd been struck, and appeared to blink back tears. "I don't know. The car drove away. There weren't any witnesses. The only person who could have answered that question was my mother."

To Ava's relief, she spotted the distinct castle ruins that marked the island of Dorsi just ahead of them in the open sea. Good. She couldn't talk about her past much longer, not without crying. And Jason Selini had already seen her unsteady and embarrassed. She wouldn't give him the satisfaction of watching her cry.

Though that seemed to be the captain's intent, with all the probing, painful questions he'd asked. What could her mother's death possibly have to do with anything? It had been months and months ago, halfway around the world. And the police had ruled it an accident.

The motor grew silent as Captain Selini slowed the boat, steering it nimbly toward the opening to a narrow inlet, past rocky cliffs that protected the secret cove. As the boat traveled around a bend to where a soft sand beach stretched out behind the rocky promontory, beyond the sight of anyone traveling past the island, the captain scowled, his eyes trained behind her.

"What?" She looked back to see what caused him to stare, but saw only the beautiful blue waves.

"I'd feel more comfortable if I knew we weren't being followed." He shook his head. The boat had already slipped past the cliffs, blocking it from the sight of anyone who might pass by the island, but also blocking their view of the sea.

"Do you really think someone could find this spot? None of those boats were close enough to see where we came in."

"They could if they were watching us with binoculars." The captain leaped onto the beach, towing a rope behind him, which he used to secure the boat to the jutting branch of a fallen tree. Then he held out his hands toward her.

Ava hesitated. She hadn't taken his hand getting into the boat, but should have. And jumping down past the lapping water onto the soft sand was vastly more difficult than stepping off a pier built for the purpose of making it easy to get on and off boats.

Reluctantly she reached for his hand. Leaning forward, she pushed off with her feet as her fingers brushed his.

"Oof!" To her dismay, in her effort to avoid hitting him, she landed with one knee in the soft sand.

"Are you okay?"

"Fine." Ava stood, brushing the sand from her knee. Realizing she wasn't hurt, she straightened and led him toward the path to the Queen's Tower. "It's this way." She hurried up the trail, the soles of her black leather walking shoes sinking deep into the sand.

The sandy trail turned to rocks as the path grew steeper, narrowing between the sheer wall of an ascending cliff on one side and the steep drop of the descending cliff on the other. Ava trusted the captain to follow her—he could surely see her footprints clearly, and once he was on the path, there wasn't anywhere else he could go. She was glad for that. Having only visited the island once, she might otherwise have had trouble finding what she sought.

A moment later the limestone tower loomed above her, and she ducked through the arched doorway into a wide stone room. The forsaken place felt cold, with sunlight penetrating only through the doorway and a couple of windows framed by thick stones. She shivered and looked back.

Jason smiled at her as he approached. Ava felt her heart lurch—with relief, of course, just relief—at seeing him still behind her. It wasn't as though her heart had any reason to be doing flip-flops at the sight of his smile. She just didn't want to be alone on the island. And Jason had saved her life. Surely whatever happiness she felt at the sight of him was due to the knowledge that he would protect her now, just as he had done earlier.

"There are stairs up to the top of the tower—it's got a glorious view of the entire island. From there we can see—"

But Jason extended his hand and cut her off. "Shh—listen."

Ava clamped her mouth closed and tried to make out any sound besides the cool wind and the hammering of her heart after the brisk climb. Wondering if perhaps the stone walls blocked outside sounds, she tiptoed toward the captain, still straining to hear. As she neared him, she detected his scent, faint but manly, reminding her of being in his arms. She shook off the memory. The man had a fine set of shoulders, she'd grant him that, but she wasn't about to waste any time wishing she was close to him. She knew better. And the man very nearly hated her.

Finally, hearing nothing, she asked, "What?"

"I thought I heard a boat motor." He shook his head. "They may have stilled the engine as they approached the island."

"No one is supposed to approach the island." Ava met his eyes and saw concern and perhaps a glimmer of fear. The captain didn't show fear often, of that she felt certain. Today had been an exception, and for good reason. "Do you think we were followed?"

"Quick." He took her hand and led her toward the arched opening to the stone stairs that led to the top of the tower. "Let's get to where we can see. If anyone's followed us, I can use my cell phone to call the guards to bring a helicopter."

Ava followed him up the stairs quickly. Hip-high parapets encircled the flat landing that towered at least twenty feet above the rest of the island. "Careful of the wall." She repeated the warning Kirk had given her on their previous visit. "Some of the old stones are loose. If you lean on them, they could fall."

In spite of her words, Jason walked close to the edge, placed one hand on the upward jut of parapet and looked back down the trail, over the treetops, toward the cove where they'd left the boat.

She marched over to stand beside him, fully intending to chide him for ignoring her warning, when she glanced in the direction where he looked, and gasped.

"A boat?" she whispered, watching through the gaps in the leafy treetops as a lone figure jumped from a second vessel. For an instant, she dared to hope the man, whose face was hidden in the shadows of a dark baseball cap, might have watched them enter the forbidden island and come to warn them the island was unsafe.

But then the man finished tying his boat next to theirs and pulled an object from his waistband. She saw it clearly through a break in the trees, just before the man bounded toward the trail they'd taken to the tower.

Ava sucked in a breath and looked up at Jason.

He'd clearly seen what the man held, too.

A gun.

SIX

Jason pulled out his phone and glanced back toward the stairs, then to the trail, thinking quickly. The gunman had no doubt seen their footprints in the sand and would have no trouble following them to the tower. The man would reach the top of the tower in two minutes or less.

Grimacing, Jason shoved his phone back into its holster. His reception was extremely low. Even if he could get a call or text to go through, there was no way the royal-guard helicopter would make it there in time. If Jason called or texted them, he'd waste valuable time.

He had to get Ava to safety.

But how would they escape the approaching gunman?

"Is there another way down from the tower?" he asked Ava in a whisper.

"Not that I know of," she admitted with a shaking voice, her words so faint he had to stand close to hear. "The only way down from the tower is the trail."

Jason cringed. He should have known better than to agree to come to the dangerous island with Ava. The last time he'd visited the place, he'd witnessed firsthand what a fall from that very tower could do to a man. Viktor Bosch, the previous head of the royal guard, had fallen to his death from the Queen's Tower. In fact, the Kevlar ropes from that very incident were still entwined around the parapets, extending down the back side of the tower past the treetops.

Crossing back to the other side of the tower, Jason scanned the trail. The gunman was already past the sand to the path that led past the cliffs. He'd reach the tower the very next minute. Jason grabbed Ava's hand, pulling her toward the back wall of the tower and taking hold of a rope with his other hand. It held securely, providing a possible means of escape. And given the circumstances, Jason was certain escape was far preferable to confrontation.

"Grab hold of this," he whispered close to her ear. "I'll help you over the edge."

"What?" Ava yelped a little too loudly. If the gunman knew for certain where they were, he'd reach them that much more quickly.

"We're going to have to rappel down the back side of the tower. There's no other way to escape."

"Can't you fight him off?"

"He's got a gun. Either or both of us could be shot."

"So we'll fall to our deaths—is that better?"

Jason hardly listened to her protests. He could hear footsteps echoing up the stone stairs from the room directly below them. In a moment the gunman would spot the steps, realize where they'd surely gone and find them. There wasn't time for Jason to send Ava over the wall and still follow her, even if she was willing to go.

"Shh," he whispered as he looped one arm securely around her slender waist. "Hold on to me."

With his other hand still tightly gripping the military-grade rope, Jason swung one leg over the wall and pulled Ava down after him.

Her whole body shuddered with a suppressed whim-

pering scream as she held tight to him. He could feel
her heartbeat racing and didn't doubt she was terrified.
He didn't feel particularly confident, either, not given
the way she wriggled with fear or the fact that the gunman would surely spot them the moment he looked over
the wall.

And he'd no doubt look over the wall.

"I need both hands to climb down." Jason found Ava's
ear and pressed his mouth close, whispering as quietly as
he dared and hoping the wind from the open sea would
bury his words instead of carrying them to the gunman.
"Hold on tight to me. I can't hold on to you."

To his relief, Ava didn't fight him, but tightened her
hold around him—one arm looped over his shoulder,
next to his neck, the other curled under his opposite arm,
so that she clung securely without choking him. Aware
the gunman could spot them at any moment, Jason began
the descent hand over hand, moving as quickly as he
dared. To his relief, the top of the tower was encircled
by jutting corbels, so that the crown projected outward
several feet beyond the stem. Once Jason had descended
far enough that they hung below the cover of the treetops
and the base of the corbels, he paused to catch his breath.

Ava, too, readjusted her grip.

"Are you okay?" he dared to whisper in a voice no
louder than a breath.

Her head bobbed silently just below his chin. She was
nodding. A good sign.

The rope shuddered in his hands.

Ava froze.

It took Jason a moment to realize what must be happening, as the rope continued to vibrate oddly, shivering
between his fingers until they swayed slightly as they
dangled from the tower.

The gunman above must have realized where they'd gone—could probably even catch a glimpse of them if he leaned over the side of the tower far enough. He couldn't shoot them because the thick stone corbels shielded them, and anyway, he didn't have to shoot. It was just as expedient to cut through the rope and let them fall to their deaths.

Jason prayed the rope would hold as he began to climb down again, the rope burning in his hands as he let them drop long stretches in a sort of controlled fall that ended up not being quite as controlled as he'd hoped. They were still ten or more feet above the uneven ground when the rope went to tatters beneath his fingers, and they half slipped, half fell to the ground.

The base of the tower was a steep slope. With Ava still clinging tightly to him, Jason caught the earth with the soles of his boots and slammed backward, sliding on his rear end down the loose gravel until he was able to dig in his heels enough to skid to a stop.

"Are you okay?" he whispered as dislodged rocks rattled down all around them.

"Fine." Ava jumped up before they'd completely stopped. She grabbed his hand and tugged him toward some trees. "This way. I know a place to hide."

Ava led the captain through the overgrown foliage toward the ruins of the cathedral. She'd looked down from the tower long enough to get her bearings. The ancient chapel was off to their right. Its roof was many centuries gone, its ceiling the open sky, but at the rear of the transept, a small door led to a back room from which the deacons of old would have entered, which Kirk had pointed out as the way he intended to enter for the wedding.

The old wooden door had long since rotted away, but thick vines curled all around that end of the building, completely covering the doorway. And the room itself had a back door that led around the apse on the east end. They could hide in the room or escape out the back.

Assuming they reached the spot before the gunman saw them.

Jason pulled her back as they cleared the edge of the trees and entered the cathedral. "Where are you going?"

"There's a room behind those vines. We can hide there."

"Not if he sees us." The captain looked behind them, peering up past the trees toward the tower.

Ava looked back, too. She could see the jutting parapets, now void of rope, but there was no sign of the gunman. "He must be on the stairs. Quick—now's our chance." She hoped to reach the hiding place before the gunman left the tower. If he'd spotted their flight through the trees, or even if he assumed they'd fallen to their deaths and went around to check, he'd be headed their way as soon as he reached the end of the trail.

Loosening his hold on her arm, Jason swept his hand down to hers and gripped her palm with a nod. "Lead the way."

Ava sprinted to the spot, fearful the gunman might try to take a shot at them as they ran through the open nave. But no gunfire sounded. She found the edge of the vines where they curled around toward the altar. The heavy mass peeled back like a curtain, and Ava pulled Jason after her as she slipped behind, pressing her hand along the cold stone wall until she found the opening to the room and ducked inside.

Sunlight filtered in dimly from a missing bit of roof far above them, but mostly the room was all thick stones and heavy vines. Ava panted, breathing freely for the first time since she'd spotted the gunman leaping off his boat.

The captain still had tight hold of her hand, and she leaned against him, her heart screaming with pent-up terror and amazement that they'd survived their fall from the tower and their flight through the trees.

It took her a few moments to begin to catch her breath as she processed all that had happened and tried to decide what they should do next. Slowly, she became aware that she'd pressed her cheek to the captain's shoulder— again. But rather than step away and draw attention to what she'd done, she pinched her eyes shut, listening for any sound of the gunman as she debated what to do next.

She didn't feel she ought to lean on Jason, but then again, the room was quite tiny and it wasn't as though she'd be able to put much space between them. Given the terror that surged through her, she felt grateful for the sense of security he provided. Quite simply, she didn't want to let go of him. Besides, she had far more important things to worry about than her proximity to the captain.

How were they going to get back to their boat without crossing paths with the gunman? Granted, the island was overgrown with trees and vines, and there were plenty of ruins to hide among, but still, the gunman had to guess they'd need to reach their boat to escape. All the man had to do was lie in wait on the trail and jump them when they tried to slip past.

Jason scowled at his phone, then whispered, "If I could get a call or text to go through, I'd use my phone to call royal-guard headquarters and have them dispatch a helicopter to the island. I'm afraid we need to get to higher ground."

"That's an excellent idea." Ava focused on the hope he offered her, refusing to be discouraged by their current lack of a phone signal. If a helicopter arrived in time, Jason's guards could apprehend the gunman, and she wouldn't have to fear for her life anymore. "I'll try to peek out and see if the way is clear." She reached toward the vines that shielded them from sight.

"Be careful." Jason's hand brushed her fingers, reminding her once again of how very close they were to each other in the tiny room and how very close they'd been. In case Ava hadn't already been convinced of the captain's strength, his climb down the rope with her clinging to him had demonstrated his capabilities quite persuasively.

She pushed those thoughts from her mind and focused on peeling back the leaves without rustling anything. For all they knew, the gunman could be just on the other side. She half expected to see the barrel of his gun pointing through the vines toward them, but as a glimmer of light filtered in through the thick foliage, she saw only the yellow limestone walls of the chapel.

Pinching one eye shut, she peered through the peephole she'd made.

"Is it clear?" Jason asked softly.

Ava startled when she spotted the gunman. She grabbed Jason's arm as he spoke, wishing he'd fall silent but not daring to make a sound to shush him. *He's there,* she mouthed, glancing at Jason for only a second before returning her attention to the gunman who'd entered the far end of the chapel.

"Try to get a good look at him," Jason told her in a faint whisper, his lips brushing her ear. "See if you recognize him."

Ava tried to ignore the shiver that ran through her

at the captain's accidental contact. She did her best to get a good look, but the leaves obscured so much of her view the man was little more than a moving shadow across the grassy floor of the cathedral ruins. She tried to guess what she could of his build, but other than her assumption he was of fairly average height and weight, there was little she could discern, certainly no distinct, identifying features.

As she watched, the man did a quick sweep of the cathedral, checking behind each ancient pillar before darting back out the way he'd come. She saw the design on his ball cap and felt her blood turn cold.

The man wore a Seattle Mariners baseball cap. She'd seen a million of the caps back home, but none since she'd been in Lydia.

The man turned away, headed in the other direction, and Ava focused on the most urgent issue.

"He's leaving," she whispered excitedly.

But Jason didn't look quite so pleased. "Is there any other way he can reach this room?"

Ava's hope fell. "If he comes around the back way." Considering what she knew of the path from the tower to the cathedral, the gunman had surely scoped out the other side of the cathedral and would loop around the back side. From there, he could go any number of directions, including through the back entrance to their tiny room.

"Show me." Jason squeezed her hand. "Is it safe?"

"We'll have to stay back. The vines aren't nearly so thick on that side." Ava led him down the narrow hallway, slowing her steps and listening as they neared the doorway on the other end. She leaned forward to look past the vines.

"Let me." Jason placed one hand on her shoulder,

stopping her, as he stepped past her and leaned forward to peer through the leaves. He blinked twice before glancing back her way, holding one finger to his lips in a gesture of silence and looking back again. She studied him as he stood there, his attention on the gunman. There was no denying the captain was handsome. Surely the odd shivers of attraction she felt toward him were superficial, nothing real or deep or lasting. She and the captain fought far too much for there to be any sort of affection between them. And she wasn't nearly ready for any more heartache in her life, not now or anytime soon.

Finally, after what felt like a much longer time than it probably was, the captain stepped back toward her.

"He's gone down the path that leads to the automated lighthouse on the north end of the island. This may be our best opportunity to make a break for it. Let's go—but be quiet. We don't know if he came to the island alone."

Ava held tight to Jason's hand as she ran after him back through the chapel and up the trail toward the royal-guard speedboat they'd left tied in the cove. Given Jason's warning about other possible gunmen loose among them, she wasn't surprised that he didn't attempt to use his phone until they reached the foot of the trail from the tower, where the trees gave way to open grass and the rocky trail turned to sand.

There he held back, ducking behind the last tree and looking at his phone. "Finally, I've got a decent signal. In case there's another gunman waiting near the boat, I'm going to call the royal guard now. We'll wait for them to arrive before we go any farther—unless we have no choice but to run for the boat. You watch back that way." He nodded his head toward the trail as he pulled out his phone and placed the call.

Ava nodded, staring back the way they'd come, alert

and watchful for any sign of movement anywhere. As she listened, Jason instructed his men to bring two helicopters to the island immediately. No sooner had he given the orders and begun to explain the reason he needed them than a movement at the top of the trail caught Ava's eye.

"Ball cap," she identified, squeezing Jason's hand. "He's back."

"We've got to go." Jason snapped his phone shut.

Ava wasn't sure whether his words were meant for her or the royal-guard dispatcher, but even as he spoke them, Jason ducked low and ran toward the boat.

"Stay close behind me," he ordered, but since he didn't let go of her hand, it wasn't as though she could have fallen far behind.

She imitated his crouching run, assuming it was some sort of tactic for staying small and providing a minimal target in case the gunman spotted him. To her amazement, they reached the boat without anyone jumping from the other craft.

Jason plucked her up by the waist and fairly threw her on board, instructing her in a quiet voice, "Stay down."

Ava did as she was told, flattening herself against the boat railing on the side nearest the island, so that anyone coming from that side wouldn't be able to see her. She hoped the boat was made of something bulletproof.

In another second Jason shoved the boat away from the shoreline with a mighty heave, sending it wide of the other vessel. He leaped aboard with the rope slung over his arm. Ava couldn't see much and didn't dare raise her head, but she assumed they must have gotten clear of the other boat, because a moment later their engine roared to life.

The boat seemed to crawl painfully through the shallow waters at first, and Ava feared they'd gotten stuck in the sand. But after a few terrified breaths, they picked up speed, clearing the narrow cove entrance and heading out to sea.

Ava panted, not so much from the run, but from her terror and amazement they'd made it free of the island without being shot. She lifted her head to say as much to Jason, but he shouted back at her, "Stay down. He's following us."

Fear lodged in her throat as the boat lurched across the waves at high speed. She imagined Jason must be engaging in some sort of evasive maneuvers as they swerved this way and that. Before long she heard Jason shouting into his phone, trying to give orders to his men over the roar of the boat and the wind and the slamming waves.

And not long after that, she heard the chop of helicopters in the air above them.

Finally. The gunman would be caught. She could go on with her wedding plans already in progress.

But she heard the captain's voice carrying over even the noise from the rotors above them.

"I don't know! I went around an island to get away from him. It's a rental boat, like the Blue Lantern rents out. Yes, I know they have dozens, but they can't all be on this stretch of sea at the same time." He paused. "I don't care if they are. Find the man. Search them all. He had a gun. He was wearing a Seattle Mariners baseball cap. Average height and build. Just find him."

Ava heard Jason identify the team on the gunman's cap and realized he must know what she knew—that the gunman probably wasn't a local.

By the time Jason finished giving orders, Ava's hope had subsided to nearly nothing.

Had they lost sight of the boat only to have it mingle

among many others? How were Jason's men supposed to search the watercraft from the sky? If they had to wait for more boats to reach the area, what were the chances they'd catch the man who'd tried to kill her?

Slim, she supposed. Slim to none.

Rather than give up completely, Ava hoped perhaps she could help identify the boat. After all, she'd seen it, however briefly. "Can I get up now?"

"Yes. Come sit up here."

When she reached the seat next to him, Jason leveled a look at her.

Already fighting unwanted feelings of attraction, she told him bluntly, "You should have fought him on the island. Then we wouldn't be in this mess."

"It was too risky."

"This is better?"

"Given how far we were from medical help, yes. If you'd been shot—if either of us had been shot—" Jason stopped trying to explain and glowered at the sea.

She'd upset him with her words. That was good. She could handle his anger far better than his embrace.

He broke the silence gruffly. "I'm going to have to hide you."

"What do you mean?"

"I mean, when I went around an island back there to get you out of range of the gunman, I lost sight of him. He didn't come around after me."

Ava frowned. She couldn't fault the captain for his attempt at keeping her from being shot—he'd achieved that objective, at least, and she was grateful for that. But at the same time, she'd hoped his men would catch her would-be killer. If the man was still at large, she wasn't safe.

Jason continued, "If the gunman headed for the marina, he could dock ahead of us and be waiting in a vehicle to see which way we go. We can't risk that."

"So you're going to have to sneak me back to the palace."

"No. I can't take you back to the palace, not if there's any chance of being followed."

"But you said the palace was the safest place in Sardis."

"It is. But my job is to protect the royal family. I can't lure a gunman to them."

The royal family. Of course. Ava swallowed as his words hit home. He didn't care nearly as much about protecting her as he cared about protecting the royal family. Somehow, as he'd held her tight on the rope and ducked into hiding with her on the island, she'd gotten it into her head that he was protecting her.

But that wasn't his job—not really. His job was to protect the royal family. She was the one endangering them. Guilt smothered her fear. What if someone got hurt because of her? She thought of the members of the royal house of Lydia she'd worked with so closely over the course of the weddings and events she'd planned. She couldn't let anything happen to them. "So you need to get rid of me?"

"I need to hide you, but you're going to have to cooperate and do as I say."

Ava nodded solemnly. This wasn't about getting her way—it was about keeping innocent people safe. "Just tell me what I need to do."

SEVEN

Jason fully expected the wedding planner to throw a fit when he docked far from the Sardis Marina, along the rocky shore north of the city, and ordered her to scramble up a muddy embankment. But to his surprise she didn't protest, not even when he offered his hand to help her out of the boat.

Granted, the woman looked shaken. In spite of the glare of the sinking sun reflecting off the water, Ava looked pale, green even, either from the jarring boat ride, her fear of the situation or a mixture of both. But instead of throwing a fit about the mud, she climbed the slippery embankment with agility, though her white pants were streaked with sludge by the time they reached the top.

Half expecting a lecture for ruining her pants, he was surprised when she instead wiped her hands on one of the few unsullied stretches of fabric and asked, "Where do I go next?"

"This way. I'll lead you." He reached for her hand.

"You can point me in the right direction if you have other places you need to be." She met his eyes with a fleeting look of challenge before quickly glancing away toward the woods.

Unsure whether he'd upset her or precisely what her

attitude change meant, Jason assured her, "It's all right. I'll take you." He led her up the path that cut along the rocky shoreline to the cluster of secluded cabins. Most of his parents' neighbors were snowbirds who'd have retreated to their northern abodes this time of year, so he wouldn't be putting them in harm's way even if Ava's enemy managed to track her to the place.

Since Jason's father had retired from the royal guard three years before, Michael and Deborah Selini had made the modest seashore retreat their year-round home. Given the location away from the city with access from the sea, and the rocky promontory that hid where he'd anchored the boat, Jason figured it was the best spot to hide the wedding planner, under the circumstances. And Jason's father often talked about how he missed being part of the royal guard.

Michael Selini would get to be a part of the action again, at least for a little while. And Jason could trust that Ava would be as safe as she could be, without luring danger back to the royal family. Jason's biggest concern was Ava's behavior. He really didn't want her snapping at his parents or getting into an argument with him in front of them. But for the moment, at least, she seemed to be stunned into silence.

He prayed she'd stay that way for a little while longer.

Jason called ahead as they made their way up the trail, so by the time they reached the house, his mother met them at the door. And though Jason had assured her the woman he was bringing by was a professional associate only, his mother's face lit up when she saw Ava was young and pretty.

And holding his hand.

Jason dropped Ava's hand and held the door for her instead. She stepped inside quickly, apologizing to Deborah for the mud on her clothes. Jason braced himself, fully expecting her to point out the mud was his fault, but instead she placed her duffel bag on the bench and silently removed her muddy shoes on the doormat.

While his mother searched through some clothes his teenage nieces had left on their last visit, Jason pulled Ava farther inside, out of view from the many porch windows. The family room, connected to the kitchen with a large fireplace in between, had only windows that looked out into the woods. "Can we close those curtains?" he asked.

His father, who'd been hovering silently since he'd first introduced himself, now got to work closing curtains, while his mother led Ava to the bathroom to change and clean up. Jason called royal-guard headquarters for an update. As he'd feared, the gunman had disappeared among the many matching boats from the same rental company. Jason kicked himself for not inspecting the boat more closely to find an identification number or a name as they'd left the island, but he'd been focused entirely on getting Ava safely beyond the gunman's range.

Now they had nothing but a list the boat-rental company had provided of the names of everyone who'd rented out a boat during the applicable time frame. There were forty-seven names and every likelihood their gunman used a fake one.

Maybe Ava was right. Perhaps he should have confronted the gunman on the island, regardless of the risks. If he'd killed or captured the man there, the royal family would arguably be safe now. So why hadn't Jason confronted him?

Surely he wasn't that worried about Ava getting hurt. Granted, hearing her story about her mother had changed his attitude toward her. He realized part of her tough exterior was likely a device for keeping her hurting heart from being further injured. But keeping the royal family safe was still a greater priority to him than worrying about Ava's safety.

His dispatcher's update didn't sit well with him.

"Investigate every one of them. I don't care if it's your own grandmother," Jason told Oliver.

"We're already on it," Oliver assured him. "And there's something more. When we briefed the evening shift on the situation, we learned a man approached the guardhouse at the pedestrian gate last evening and asked after Ava Wright."

"What? Who? Do we have surveillance footage of this man?"

"I've pulled up the footage from the two cameras that cover the guard booth and his approach from across the street. Unfortunately his baseball cap was pulled low and covered most of his face, given that the cameras are mounted above."

Jason let out a disappointed breath. "Any other identifying features?"

"Dark hair. Average height, average build."

"What exactly did he say?"

"He asked if Ava Wright was around. Since she'd already returned to her apartment for the evening, the men told him she wasn't. He turned and left. That's all."

"Save that footage. I want to see it when I come in."

"Of course. When will you be in?"

Jason hesitated, torn. From the sound of it, his men had everything under control—there wasn't anything he could do that wasn't already being done. Besides not wanting to burden his parents with taking care of Ava alone, he had more questions he needed to ask her. The circumstances surrounding her mother's death seemed more than fishy, but Ava wouldn't like his questions, not given what he needed to ask. It might take him a while to get the answers he needed.

"I'm not sure, Oliver. There's more going on here than what we've learned. I'm going to try to sort out the details, but it seems—" he raked his hair back as he tried to choose his words judiciously "—we're up against a determined killer."

With a few words of encouragement, Jason ended the call, still mulling over his choice of words. Normally, given that the attempts on Ava's life hadn't succeeded, he'd have referred to their enemy as an attempted murderer. But from what he'd learned so far, it seemed most likely the man who was after Ava had successfully killed before and wouldn't back off until he'd killed again.

As Jason explained the situation and hashed out security issues with his father, Ava exited the bathroom, the jagged stripes of her zebra-print top replaced with a pink kitten-adorned T-shirt. She'd traded her once-crisp white slacks for a pair of worn, oversize blue jeans, and soft baby-blue slipper-socks covered her feet. Her hair had fallen into limp curls after the wind and sea spray had finished with it. Ava had obviously tried to comb them flat, but already they were drying into floppy curls that framed her wide eyes, softening her usually severe look.

Gone was her makeup, too. Instead of her usual war paint, Ava's cheeks danced with freckles, and her pale pink lips looked fuller without the usual dark red veneer. She looked up at him with uncertainty in her eyes, all the usual fight gone, along with her perennial glare.

Jason smiled at her. He told himself he needed to be friendly, especially given the questions he was soon to ask and how they were certain to upset her. But also, he realized with odd fascination, Ava didn't look like her usual self. She looked more like the pretty girl in the picture he'd found on her desk.

Ava caught her lower lip in her teeth and glanced around, clearly out of her element. This wasn't a wedding. She wasn't in charge. In fact, she was surrounded by Selinis.

Just as Jason stepped toward her, his mother pulled her head out from where she'd been rummaging in the refrigerator.

"Have you had supper? Can I get you something to eat?" Deborah asked.

"That's so sweet of you. I hate to be a bother." Ava offered the woman a strained half smile. "Something warm, perhaps? I can't stop shivering."

The summer evening hadn't cooled much, but Jason suspected Ava's chill came from the threats against her life and her fear of what would happen next.

While his mother began fixing a bowl of soup and a warm cup of tea for the wedding planner, Jason grabbed the duffel bag she'd left in the enclosed porch. "I'd like to look at these documents more closely. Can you join me?"

His mom shooed them out of the kitchen while she heated their soup and tea. Ava followed Jason to the family room, where his father occupied the large recliner. His mother's chair was positioned on the other side of his father's, nearest the kitchen. Ava hesitated between the sofa and the chair.

Jason led her to the couch. "Sorry. You'll have to sit beside me."

Though Ava hesitated, she didn't protest but picked up one of the pillows that leaned against the sofa arm, then perched in its spot, clutching the pillow tight to her chest as she watched him with wide eyes.

Guilt swirled inside him. He reminded himself he'd

done his best, and fortunately kept her safe thus far, but that didn't change the fact that he'd soon be asking her very difficult questions. He'd have to choose his words wisely.

Ava watched Jason lower himself onto the sofa beside her. "Does your back hurt?" She realized he'd been hit plenty hard by the car that morning. No doubt rappelling down the tower and falling to the rocky ground below hadn't helped any.

"What's wrong with your back?" Jason's father asked before the captain could answer.

"He got hit by a car this morning," Ava answered when Jason merely shrugged and winced.

While Jason's mom shrieked and tutted from the kitchen, quizzing him on how badly he'd been hit and whether he'd gone straight to the doctor, Michael Selini got up from his chair. "I'll get you a heat pack for that. Do you want any painkillers?"

"Of course he needs painkillers," Deborah insisted while Jason reluctantly agreed.

"I need to talk to the wedding planner," Jason reminded his parents.

His father brought him pills and a mug of tea, then returned with a mug for Ava and a warmed heat pack for Jason's back. Jason adjusted the pack several times, but it kept sliding off.

"Here. Let me help." Ava picked up the fallen bag. "Where do you want it?"

"Middle back. Up a little. To the left," Jason directed her as she adjusted the bag.

She found she had to scoot closer to him to reach around his wide shoulders. That brought her knees next to his and their faces close enough she could see the five-o'clock shadow sprouting on his chin. How had she never before noticed how handsome he was? The man had a fine, angular jaw. And though his glare could be commanding, his gray eyes sparkled with concern and compassion and...other things she shouldn't be thinking about.

Jason was an excellent captain of the guard with an important job to do. It was her fault he'd been injured and had been forced to do so many brave things just to keep her safe. In fact, she felt awful that he was with her now, instead of back at headquarters with his men, protecting the royals as he was supposed to.

She vowed to cooperate with his questions and not keep him any longer from his work. More than that, she pondered what she ought to do. By rights, she ought to leave Lydia to lure her would-be killer away from the royal family, instead of closer to them. But with Alexander's wedding just over a week away, she'd only be leaving them in the lurch if she tried to flee now. They needed her there for the wedding to go smoothly.

Nor could they postpone the event. International dignitaries were planning to attend. They'd made their reservations. All of Lydia had prepared to host them, with hotels adding rooms and restaurants adding staff in preparation for the deluge of guests and the boon to the tourism industry. On top of that, the media had already descended on the town, reporting on each foreign dignitary as he or she arrived, and speculating on what the cake and the dress might look like.

Without Ava, the event would be an internationally broadcast flop. She couldn't leave. But she also couldn't stand the thought that harm might come to the royals because of her.

Jason's parents brought them mugs of soup, then disappeared outside, with Michael insisting on walking the perimeter and Deborah refusing to let him go alone. As the door closed behind them, Ava realized she couldn't hold the heat pack on Jason's back and eat her soup at the same time.

"It's okay. My back feels better already."

She placed the heat pack on the glass-topped coffee table and tasted the soup, a spicy Mediterranean chicken with large chunks of vegetables. "This is delicious. It was very kind of your mother to go out of her way—I hope I'm not endangering them by being here."

"They're glad to do it," Jason hastily assured her. "I doubt we've been followed. My guess is that the gunman was entirely focused on hiding from the helicopters, not on following us. We'll wait awhile to make sure he doesn't show up. If everything stays quiet here, I'll have the guard send a car for us, preferably while it's still dark. They can take a roundabout route to throw off anyone who might follow them."

"That sounds like a wise plan." Ava sipped another spoonful of soup.

Jason raised an eyebrow and watched her warily.

"What?" she asked.

"You haven't yelled at me in a while."

"I really don't yell that often." She defended herself, quickly reviewing her patterns. Yes, there were times when she got snippy with vendors, especially when they tried to pass off inferior products, but she never yelled at any member of the wedding party. "You usually provoke me."

Jason scowled.

Ava analyzed her claim. Did the captain of the guard really provoke her that much? Or did she deliberately push him away, even more than she pushed others?

Maybe it was because he was an authority figure who often defied her. Or perhaps she *had* noticed how handsome he was, but told herself otherwise because she didn't want to admit she might be attracted to him.

Finally, in a small voice, she offered, "I'm sorry."

"It's not your fault someone's trying to kill you."

"Not that. I'm sorry for that, too, but I meant that I'm sorry to have yelled at you." As she spoke the words, she realized just how much she meant them. Her thoughts flooded with the memory of clinging to Jason as he carried her down the rope on the island—of how terrified she'd felt because of the gunman, but how safe Jason had kept her. How could she have yelled at this man? He'd dived in front of a speeding car for her. If she'd doubted for a moment the impact of his selflessness, she only had to recall how the car had dented his body armor.

He'd risked so much for her.

"Don't cry," Jason begged.

Only then did Ava realize tears were flowing freely down her cheeks. "I'm sorry. I'm fine. Really, I'm fine." She set her soup on the coffee table and swiped at the tears with her hands.

Jason pulled the towel from around the heat pack and handed it to her. "You're not fine, but that's perfectly understandable given what you've been through today."

She clamped the cloth against her eyelids as though she could force the tears back. "I'm not the one who's been through so much. You were hit by a car."

"What's that?"

Ava realized the towel had muffled her words. She peeked past it and met his eyes. "You were hit by a car. You could have been killed."

Jason looked back at her with apology on his face. She wasn't sure how she expected him to respond to her tearful apology, but she certainly wasn't expecting his resigned words, spoken in a grim voice. "I need to ask you a question."

"What?"

"Did your mother have a life-insurance policy?"

Ava swallowed. His words seemed to come from nowhere, and yet...her mother had been killed, hit by a car. Someone had tried to hit Ava with a car. The events were similar, but Ava didn't see what insurance had to do with any of it. She answered hesitantly, though she was sure of her answer. "Yes."

"Who was the beneficiary?"

"My father and me. But we haven't gotten anything yet. The insurance company has it all tied up in court. There was a clause against suicide. They claim my mother stepped out in front of an oncoming car, deliberately."

Jason nodded solemnly. "How much was the policy worth?"

"Half a million dollars. That may sound like a lot of money, but it's fairly standard, hardly exorbitant. She qualified for a low rate because of her excellent health." Ava quoted all she could remember, still not seeing clearly why Jason wanted to know. Unless... "You don't think she was hit on purpose, do you?"

EIGHT

Jason clenched his jaw, hating the conversation, hating the pain that stretched across Ava's freckled face as she realized the reasoning behind his questions. He didn't know what more to say, not without causing her further pain.

She leaned away from him and shook her head slowly. "No. No. The only people who'd have any reason to do that—" Her voice caught, and she pressed the towel to her eyes again.

"How viable was your mother when your father withdrew life support?"

Ava shook her head, red color flushing to her face as she lowered the towel and stood on shaking feet. "No. My father didn't kill my mother."

"Isn't that what you accused him of?" Jason recalled her words clearly, their meaning too stark for him to soon forget.

"I didn't mean it like that." She flung the towel down on the coffee table and walked toward the door.

Jason didn't know where she intended to go, but he couldn't let her leave, not when a killer was out there somewhere, searching for her, hoping to finish the job. "Ava." He caught her arm.

She fought to move past him.

He blocked her way, wrapping his arms around her as she tried to step around him, holding her tight as she fought him.

"I need to go. I need fresh air." Her voice rose to a panicked note. "I can't look at you right now. How could you suggest— You don't know my father. He's a minister. He loved my mom."

"You're right. I don't know." Jason held her tight against him as she struggled to get away. If she left the cabin, especially distraught as she was right now, she'd be an easy target, never mind that she would have no idea how to navigate the twisting roads through the foothills back to town. "I don't know why anyone would try to kill you, either, but someone is."

Ava tried a moment longer to twist away; then the fight stilled from her slowly as her efforts gave way to sobbing. She pressed her face against his shoulder. "He wouldn't," she whispered, then sagged downward so that Jason had to support all her weight just to keep her upright.

Unsure what else to do, but certain he ought to try to comfort her, he rubbed her back gently and thought frantically for something to say. But what was there? Someone had tried to kill her with a car bomb that morning. When that hadn't worked, he'd tried to run her down with a car. If the killer had succeeded in a hit-and-run before, it would make sense he'd fall back on that plan when his first attempt failed.

Determined to ease her agony, though he didn't know what else he could possibly do to comfort her, Jason asked, "Can I pray with you?"

Ava shuddered against him, not answering at first. Finally she turned her face so that his shoulder no longer muffled her words. "No. God doesn't listen. He doesn't care about me." She choked back tears and buried her face in his shoulder again.

Jason simply held her, too stunned to know what to say. He'd watched her in action at enough weddings of the Christian royal family, as she'd paid lip service to God and said all the right things, he'd assumed she was a person of faith. Her father was a minister, after all, and she'd grown up in the church.

He pulled her closer to him and rubbed her back again, mulling over this newfound surprise. The bitterness behind her words seemed to indicate that Ava had tried praying before, but somehow, instead of finding comfort in the midst of her painful experiences, she had lost her faith. Jason's mouth felt dry. What could he do? She didn't want him to pray with her.

Instead he pinched his eyes shut, held her tight in his arms and prayed silently for her, that God would ease her suffering, that she'd be willing to receive God's comfort, if she could. And that somehow they'd stop the killer who was after her, before he struck again.

The prayer rose in Jason's heart without words, fueled by determination and compassion, and something else he hadn't expected to feel, not around the fiery wedding planner. Something akin to affection, more than friendly concern. Somewhere, buried deep beneath the spiked armor and the prickly words, Ava had a tender heart that had been hurt, badly.

Without meaning to, he thought of the smiling picture of the Ava some time ago. He'd never seen her smile in real life. The prayer surged up from his heart that God would heal the hurt inside Ava. That she could smile again.

* * *

Ava clung to the captain of the guard, burying her face against his strong shoulder as she struggled to fight down the hurt that surged inside her after everything she'd endured already—her fiancé's betrayal, the loss of her best friend, moving halfway around the globe and starting over, the attempts on her life—and now this.

No matter how much she wanted to believe her father couldn't—wouldn't—do anything to hurt her mother, she couldn't deny the validity of Jason's concerns, especially coupled with the attempt on her life that morning, the glaring "coincidence" between her mother's death and the attempted hit-and-run.

Much as she wished she could scream at Jason that it couldn't be true, she didn't have the heart to protest. His theory made sense. Painful, hideous sense.

And besides that, she couldn't bring herself to scream at Jason again, not when he'd stared her down through so many arguments and still had the heart to hold her right now. Without his support, she'd droop to a sobbing puddle on the floor. The simple fact was, like it or not, she needed him right now, just as she'd needed his help on the island and his daring bravery on the street in front of her apartment.

Maybe she'd always needed him.

The thought came out of nowhere, filtering through her pain like a fragrant balm, easing her unbearable sadness. This man, this strong, handsome man, had treated her far better than she deserved to be treated. He'd been patient and thoughtful. Granted, he'd yelled right back at her more times than she could count, but she'd goaded him on.

And he'd always fought fair.

With jagged gulps, Ava pulled in deep breaths, trying to calm herself. She realized Jason was rubbing her back with gentle, soothing motions. How long had he been doing that? She didn't know, but gratitude filled her heart. The man treated her so much better than she deserved, apparently out of the sheer goodness of his heart, since his real duty was to the royals.

She peeled her face away from his tear-soaked uniform shirt and looked him full in the face.

"You going to be okay?" he asked her warily.

She nodded, still not trusting her voice.

"Good. I'd like to get back to headquarters. We've got security footage of a man who approached the pedestrian gatehouse last evening and asked about you. I want you to see if you recognize him. Are you up for that?"

If it meant a possible break in the case, Ava was up for anything. "Sure. Is it safe to leave?"

"I'll call for a car. It will take them at least an hour to get here. We still have time to finish our soup."

As they waited for the car to arrive and Jason's parents to return, Ava finished her soup slowly, staring at the pictures on the cabin walls almost without seeing. Jason made some phone calls, then joined her as she stood before a large collage of photographs that dominated one wall.

"Are these all family members?" she asked, hoping to talk about something—anything—less painful than the possibility that her father might have killed her mom and even turned on her.

"Yeah. We're a big family. My parents had five daughters before I came along. They're all married and their kids are nearly grown now. These are mostly of my nieces and nephews." He led her toward the hallway, where an older collage bore pictures of a much-younger

Jason. "Here's where my mom keeps the embarrassing shots of me."

Ava looked with wonder at the goofy boy doing headstands on the sofa, standing proudly next to a dirt bike, grinning at the camera from between his sisters, with pink bows in his hair. She pointed at the snapshot and laughed.

"My oldest sister wanted to be a hairstylist. She liked to practice on me."

"It's a good look for you," she teased. "Your sister knew what she was doing." She glanced at Jason, expecting a snappy retort or possibly embarrassment, but instead the look on his face made her breath catch in her throat.

Ava was smiling. Laughing, even. Jason stared as the smile brightened her face from the inside, transforming her appearance. She really was the same person as the pretty girl in the picture on her desk, wasn't she? But unlike an old two-dimensional photo, she was so much more stunning in real life.

And resilient. Not that he'd expected her to keep crying nonstop, but she'd put her pain away and turned her attention to happier things. It seemed a well-practiced move. But then, if she'd buried her mother a week before she'd arrived in Lydia, she'd obviously had to learn to ignore her pain and put on a brave face.

Her sternness over the past several months now made more sense. In fact, he felt a little in awe of her, that she'd served the royal family so faithfully through many happy family occasions, while at the same time silently mourning the tragic loss of her mother. Just as inspiring was the smile she flashed him, however quickly it disappeared. Instantly, Jason felt the old challenge returning.

Growing up, he'd been the family clown, the little boy who could make everyone laugh. Then he'd been the class clown. One smile could goad him to bring on a hundred more, until his father, fed up with his foolishness, had sent him off to a military youth camp to toughen up.

He'd gotten plenty tough, risen to every challenge and fought his way to the very top, to the captain's desk that had always evaded his father. But he made very few people laugh from behind the captain's desk. It had been a long time since he'd bothered trying to make anyone smile.

And maybe there wasn't much sense attempting to make Ava laugh again, not tonight when so many concerns plagued them, but someday. He'd like to see her smile again.

How long he stood there, lost in thought, watching Ava, he wasn't sure. He heard stomping outside, and voices. "Sounds like my parents are back," he murmured and turned to the door.

His parents reported all was clear outside.

"I can take the boat back to the marina for you," his father offered. "We don't want to leave it in the cove until morning. If anyone spots it, it won't take them long to find the trail to the house."

Jason agreed. "Good plan. I've called for a car to come pick us up." He updated his folks on everything that had been decided. While he handed over the speedboat keys and explained to his father the difference between this newer model and the boats his father had driven in previous years, Ava joined his mother in the kitchen.

Deborah chatted with Ava amiably. Jason listened with only half an ear, focused mostly on his conversation with his father, but when he heard his mother mention to Ava for the third time that she was welcome to visit again, he decided he ought to intervene.

"Mom, can you give me a hand in the back closet?"

"Sure." His mother followed him. "What do you need?"

"I need you to help me find something."

They left Ava behind in the kitchen. When they reached the closet, his mother asked, "What are you looking for?"

"A moment's privacy." He gave his mother an apologetic look. "Could you please refrain from inviting the wedding planner back to the house?"

"It's too late for that."

"She's not some girl I've brought by to meet you and Dad."

"She is a girl, we've met her and we like her—"

"You don't really know her."

"Do you really know her?"

"Hardly."

"Perhaps you should get to know her. You're thirty-three, Jason. I'll have great-grandchildren before you get married, if you ever get married to anything besides your job—"

Jason had long sensed he'd inherited his argumentative nature from his sometimes-stubborn mother. "Have you been listening, Mother? Ava's life is in danger. This is hardly the time—"

But his mother only patted his hand and cut off his words. "Your father and I arrived back from our walk in silence. We saw the two of you gazing at each other—"

"We weren't gazing!"

"Oh? What would you call it?"

Jason wasn't sure what he would call it, since he wasn't entirely certain what they had been doing. He'd been lost in thought, considering things he hadn't contemplated in years, things he probably didn't need to be thinking about right now given all the more pressing details they had to worry about.

His mother continued, "You didn't hear us until we made a lot of noise. Whatever the two of you were doing, you were quite wrapped up in each other."

"I've got a job to do." Jason turned to leave.

"You asked me for help, Jason."

"That was an excuse to get you away from the wedding planner."

"I think you need my help more than you care to admit."

"I don't—"

"Give this girl a chance. Get to know her."

"She's an American. She'll probably want to return to the States—"

"Not if you give her a reason to stay."

Jason stared at his mother in wonderment. How many times had he and Ava argued? He was sure he couldn't stand the woman. And yet the more he got to know her, the more he wondered if all those arguments hadn't been fueled, at least in part, by a desire to stomp down an unwanted sense of attraction. Whatever it was about the woman that got his blood boiling, his mother had picked up on it. He wished he knew what it was. "Why her?"

"She trusts you."

"I honestly doubt that." Jason could think of a dozen things Ava had said that would indicate she didn't trust him at all.

"I saw more than you realize," his mother told him flatly. "That girl looks up to you. From what I understand, she needs a friend right now, maybe even more than she needs a guard."

Jason wished he could think of a sharp retort, but his mother's words struck home.

"I know you intend to keep her safe, Jason, but promise me you won't let her get hurt."

Confused, Jason asked, "What do you mean?"

"She's afraid of many things right now. Her heart is vulnerable. Don't hurt her."

Jason started to leave.

"Here." His mother pulled a women's jacket from a hanger. "It's getting cool outside. You said you needed my help with something in the closet."

"Right." Jason grinned, shaking his head as he took the jacket. "Thanks for your help."

As he stepped back into the family room, Ava turned to him, her eyes wide, questioning. He held out the jacket to her and she gave him a grateful smile.

"I was feeling chilly." She slipped it on. "How thoughtful of you." Though her eyes looked wary, when she looked up at him, Jason saw the look his mother had identified. Ava trusted him.

But with all the possible pitfalls that lay ahead, could he prove himself worthy of that trust?

NINE

Ava closed her eyes during the long car drive back into the city. She wished she could rest, but her head spun with a thousand questions, not just about her mother's death and the attacks against her, but also about the wedding so quickly approaching and how she could possibly be involved without endangering the lives of everyone who attended.

But more than all those questions, which ought to have been foremost on her mind, Ava couldn't shake the feeling of being in Jason's arms as he'd soothed her while she cried. When was the last time anyone had held her like that? She'd refused to face her father after her mother's death. Dan, her fiancé, had held her close as they'd buried her mother. She'd thought she could trust him.

And then? She'd returned from Queen Monica's vow-renewal ceremony to discover how Dan had warded off loneliness in her absence. Her heart pinched at the memory. How could any man hold her close one day and then betray her so deeply not many days later?

She glanced at Jason, sitting in the front passenger seat, as he barked orders into his phone. He was clearly frustrated by the many dead ends they'd hit, and determined to find answers in spite of their lack of clues.

Her heart swirled with questions. Was she foolish to trust this man? In the wake of Dan's betrayal, she'd pushed away everyone who might have gotten close to her wounded heart. But months had passed, and time had eased the hurt. Was she strong enough to trust again? Maybe. Looking at Jason's strong profile against the starlight beyond the windows, she wanted so very much to put her faith in him.

But he'd only ever fought her before. The paradox taunted her. Perhaps feeling affection for Jason was just asking for trouble. He'd given her little reason to believe she meant anything special to him. That he'd rubbed her back while she cried might have been only an impatient attempt to calm her so they could talk. It met his objectives as the captain of the guard.

Surely she ought to take a step back and think clearly about the situation before she let her feelings run away with her. But then again, as Jason glanced into the backseat, met her eyes and offered her a small, encouraging smile, she wondered if it wasn't already too late.

Jason ushered Ava into the royal-guard headquarters, heading straight for the conference room, where their largest, high-definition screen would give him the best view of the surveillance image of the man who'd inquired after her the evening before. Oliver joined them, warning them as he brought up the image, "I'm afraid we didn't get much."

Prepared though he was, Jason couldn't help feeling disappointed. He wasn't at all surprised when Ava shook her head. "There's not enough showing of his face for me to recognize anything. Just a bit of jawline, some dark hair. He could be bald under that ball cap for all we know."

To his chagrin, the man's jacket and slacks looked utterly generic, nor did the man have any jewelry or tattoos on display. The closest thing they had to a personal clue was the distinctive compass-emblazoned *S* on his cap.

"That's a Seattle Mariners cap, same as the gunman who attacked us on the island," Jason noted.

Ava seemed extremely reluctant to consider the direction the clue pointed. "Most of the men in Seattle have a cap like that."

"Most?"

"At least half."

"But this isn't Seattle."

"No, but even if the gunman didn't come from my hometown, it's common knowledge I'm from Seattle. He could have bought a cap anywhere and worn it to throw us off the real trail."

Jason suspected Ava only wanted to believe the man hadn't followed her from home. Still, he couldn't prove otherwise, nor could he discredit her theory completely. He turned his attention to what they knew. "He's average height, average build. Same as the gunman who came after us on the island."

"And the gunman wore similar clothing. The two were probably the same man."

Jason had another question he needed to ask, but he didn't want to pose it to Ava just yet, not when he feared it might provoke tears. "It's late. You need your rest. Can I walk you to the apartment?"

Ava shook her head. "You need your rest, too. I'm sure one of your men can walk me over." She turned toward the hallway.

Jason watched her in wonderment. Was this the same woman who'd refused a guard that morning? She'd told him then she didn't think his guards liked her. He couldn't argue with her claim. In fact, knowing that his guards viewed her with much the same resentment he'd felt until that evening, he didn't want them walking her home. They would still think she was the argumentative wedding planner.

They wouldn't know about the real Ava with the tender heart and who had such a pretty smile, reserved only for those who knew how to coax it out of hiding. He trotted to catch up with her and caught the duffel bag that sagged from her shoulders, falling into step beside her.

"Really, I'm fine, thank you," she told him, reaching for the bag.

"It's not far."

"You have important things to do."

Though he didn't want to mention it, Jason confessed, "I have a question to ask you."

She stopped by the rear exit door. "You can ask me now."

"I'd rather not."

She pushed through the door, holding it open so he could step after her. "You're making me a little nervous. You know how I feel about your questions."

"I'm afraid you won't like this one any more than the last, but it has to be asked. I just didn't want to ask it in the middle of headquarters."

Walking briskly, they reached the rear door of the palace-wall apartments, and Jason pressed his thumb to the print pad, which registered green, allowing them entrance. He opened the door for her.

"How thoughtful of you," she said, only realizing as she looked around the small apartment just how thoughtful he'd been. Someone had brought by her things from her apartment.

"I told the men to be careful with everything. And don't worry, Theresa lent me some girls from house-keeping to pack and unpack your personal things. The men just did the heavy lifting and kept the ladies safe."

"I appreciate that." Ava had already begun to worry about getting her work done without her computer and printer, but she saw these, along with her desk, had been set up just as she'd had them. Appreciation swelled inside her, but she knew their discussion wasn't over. "Ask your question."

"Could the man in the footage have been your father?"

Ava closed her eyes. Her features pinched slowly as she struggled to answer. She gave him the tiniest nod, but when she opened her mouth, her voice caught.

"It's okay." Jason rushed to assure her. "You don't have to say it out loud. I understand."

But her face pinched up all the more, and she sagged forward, shaking her head adamantly. "I don't want to believe he's capable of something like this."

"I don't want to think so, either. And I truly hope he isn't, but given the circumstances, it's a possibility we can't ignore." Jason was tempted to put an arm around her again, to comfort her in her obvious distress, but his mother's words echoed in his thoughts. Ava trusted him. He didn't want to hurt her and wasn't sure he ought to hold her when he didn't know what the next day might bring.

Instead he asked the next logical question. Though it was almost midnight in Lydia, it would be midafternoon back in Seattle. If they called Ava's father and caught him in his office in the U.S., Jason would know the man couldn't possibly have been behind the attacks that day. "Can you call your father?"

Ava looked up at him, and he quickly explained his reasoning.

"It's a good idea," she admitted. "But I haven't spoken to him since my mother's death. I'm already too emotional. If he answers he'll want to know what's going on." She shook her head. "I'm not up to it. Not now. Not after the day we've had."

"It's fine," Jason assured her. "Do you mind if I call him?"

Ava looked sincerely relieved by his suggestion. "Please." She wrote down two phone numbers for her father, labeling them Home and Office.

"Would you like me to place the call from my office and leave you alone?"

"I don't think I could sleep not knowing." She slipped the paper into his hand and clung to his fingers an extra-long moment.

Jason noticed. He tried not to call attention to that fact and debated whether he should hold her hand or pull away. He'd need to dial the phone. "I'll call right now."

Ava dropped his hand, and Jason punched in the first phone number. It rang several times, but there was no answer, not even a machine or voice mail. He dialed the second number.

The church secretary answered, and Jason asked if he could speak to Pastor Wright.

"I'm sorry, he's out of the office right now. May I take a message?"

"Do you know when he'll be back?"

"I can't say."

"Are you expecting him in tomorrow?"

"Tomorrow is Saturday. The office will be closed."

Right. "Can you tell me when would be a good time to reach him? Or do you have another number I could call?"

"If you could tell me your message or reason for calling, perhaps I could help you."

Jason thought quickly. What could he tell the woman that would get him the answer he wanted, without giving away too much, especially if Ava's father really was their culprit? But then again, even if the minister learned they'd called, what difference would it make? Perhaps they could just as well flush him out by identifying themselves.

With a silent prayer that he wasn't making a big mistake, Jason explained, "I'm the captain of the royal guard of the kingdom of Lydia. Pastor Wright's daughter is our royal wedding planner."

"Is everything all right?" The secretary jumped in when Jason paused. "Is Ava okay?"

"She's fine," Jason assured the woman, hoping he wasn't giving away too much. "We had some questions for her father, if you could leave a message for him to call us back."

"Oh, yes, certainly." The woman took down the number for the royal guard's main switchboard, as well as Jason's personal cell-phone number. Then she quickly added, "Tell Ava we miss her. I miss her smiling face and all the insightful things she used to say during Bible study. I do hope she's fine. She's such a sweet girl. I've been praying for her ever since—since her mother died."

"She is fine," Jason noted, and then, on impulse, since the secretary had brought it up, he added, "Keep praying for her. She has a lot going on right now."

As he spoke, he saw Ava's face go white. He closed the call and put the phone away.

"You didn't need to say that." Ava looked up at him angrily.

"She told me she's been praying for you," Jason explained.

"Now she'll worry for no reason." Ava threw her hands up in the air—a signal, Jason had learned long before, that she was ready to argue and wouldn't back down until she'd won the fight.

"For no reason?" he repeated, not bothering to list the many reasons Ava and everyone who cared for her ought to worry about her safety.

"There's nothing she can do about it from there."

"She can pray for you. You need all the prayer you can get." Jason didn't want to argue, but Ava had made it clear she wasn't going to let him get away without a fight.

"It doesn't work," Ava told him tartly, glaring up at him. "I prayed for my mother. And I believed, stupidly, that God was with me, that God loved me even though my mother died."

Jason listened, surprised. He would have sworn Ava had buried her faith the moment her mother had taken her last breath. But her words indicated she'd held on longer than that. He wanted to ask her to clarify, to explain the precise moment she'd lost her faith and why. But he realized it wasn't any of his business, and he feared such a question would only push her further away. He didn't dare risk that, not when he already saw her rebuilding the walls around her heart even higher than before.

"I'm tired." Ava walked to the door and held it open for him. "Good night."

He crossed the room obediently, but turned to face her in the doorway. "I don't want to see you hurt."

"Then leave before I cry."

"Ava." He reached for her, his heart breaking from the pain she carried.

But she swatted him away and closed the door after him. He heard the tumbler of the dead bolt slide solidly into place. He still had her duffel bag of papers slung over his shoulder and half expected her to reopen the door just to grab it from him. He waited.

How long he stared at the door, he couldn't say, but he prayed she'd open it and let him in. When enough time passed that it didn't seem likely she'd change her mind, he prayed instead she'd open the door of her heart to God. God could comfort her far more than Jason could, if only she'd let him.

Jason trudged back to his office and set the duffel bag on his desk, zipping it open, praying for answers. It was late and he was tired, but at the same time, he didn't feel he could sleep, not yet. Riffling through the brochures, Jason spotted one with Ava's smile, her hair still a natural, wavy brown as she stood between a beaming wedding couple and their cake.

It was the brochure for the wedding-planning company Ava had run back in the U.S. Jason realized he didn't know what had become of the company. Curious, he dialed the number on the brochure. It was still business hours back in Ava's hometown.

"Happily Ever After," a woman answered in a cheerful voice. "How may I help you plan the wedding of your dreams?"

"I'm calling about Ava Wright."

"I'm sorry, she's no longer with our company."

Jason scrambled to think what he could ask next that wouldn't make the woman concerned, just as Ava had accused him of upsetting her father's secretary. "Actually, that's why I'm calling. I'm on the staff of the Lydian royal family. Everyone here is very impressed with her work." He paused, recalling his conversation with his mother and the question he'd raised whether Ava might be planning to return to the U.S. Perhaps this woman could answer more than one question.

"We're hoping to keep her on staff full-time," Jason continued, trusting his words weren't a lie. From everything he'd seen, the royals would love to have Ava work for them, planning events long into the future. "Could you fill me in on her relationship with your company? Is she planning to return?"

"Oh, I'm sure she's not—though I wish she would. I miss her. But considering the circumstances that surrounded her leaving…" The woman's voice trailed off.

"What were those circumstances? She's never spoken of them to us."

"No, I don't suppose she would." The woman gave a short laugh. "I can't say I know everything—no one ever bothered to explain it all to me, but I'm just the secretary. She broke off her engagement so suddenly just before she left."

Ava had been engaged? Suddenly Jason had a dozen new questions. "Why did she end her engagement? Was that before her first trip to Lydia?"

"It was after she returned—the one time she returned. I probably shouldn't discuss it—I don't even know what happened. Dan did something—"

"Her fiancé's name was Dan?"

"Yes, Dan. Daniel Johnson. I don't know what he did to upset her, but she handed over the company to her partner and walked away. Oh, and she changed her hairstyle. She stopped smiling. It was as though something snapped inside her. I wish I could tell you more, but that's all I know."

Jason jotted down the man's name. "Thank you, you've been very helpful."

"If you see her, could you tell her Myra says hello? And I wish her every happiness."

"Happiness?" Jason repeated the word.

"Yes. She's brought so much happiness to everyone else, I just wish she could find some herself. She wasn't happy when she left, but if anyone deserves to live happily ever after, she does."

Stunned by the woman's sudden outpouring, Jason didn't know what to say. "I'll pass along your greetings," he promised.

"Thank you." Myra sounded somewhat emotional, so Jason thanked her again for her help and ended the call.

He put away his phone, pondering this new element to the mystery. Who was Dan Johnson, and what had he done that had caused Ava to abandon a successful company, change her hairstyle and move halfway around the world? And why hadn't Ava mentioned the man before? Given the circumstances, Jason considered Dan a person of interest. Clearly, the man had hurt Ava before. Who was to say he wasn't trying to do so again?

With little more to go on than the man's name—and a common name, at that—Jason decided to place a query with the Lydian travel authorities. Given the late hour, he sent out an email to the airports, the border crossings and the marina. It wasn't much of a net. There were plenty of ways a man who wanted to hide might slip through.

But at the same time, it was the only thing Jason could think to do without waking Ava and grilling her about why she'd neglected to mention anything about the man. Dissatisfied but unable to do any more, he headed home to catch a few hours' sleep. He'd be back at his office early the next morning. He prayed by then he'd have some answers.

TEN

Ava did not want to get up the next morning. Her dreams hadn't been anything too nice, but they were far preferable than the nightmare her life had become. But since she had a meeting with the palace kitchen staff and the bakery that was providing the cake, she had no choice but to get up. She might endanger the royal family with her presence, but there wasn't any helping that. She could, however, make good on her promise to give Prince Alexander's bride, Lillian, the wedding of her dreams.

They'd arranged to hold the food meeting in the grand ballroom, which was there inside the palace, so she had no excuse not to attend. She pulled herself out of bed the moment the alarm went off and tried to wash away every hint of the previous day's trials in the shower. Red rimmed her eyes, but she'd had plenty of practice putting in eyedrops to whiten them—not only on members of her wedding parties, but also for herself. And she styled her hair extra high to detract attention from her face and eyes. It was a simple ruse, but it worked remarkably well.

The early-morning meeting went smoothly. Fortunately she'd worked with the same bakery for Princess Isabelle's wedding and Duchess Julia's titling ceremony, so everyone knew what to expect. There were no surprises. Ava took a deep, calming breath as she thanked everyone for meeting with her and turned to leave the ballroom. A sense of tentative peace settled over her. Perhaps today would be a better day.

Then she spotted Captain Selini standing in the doorway, his uniform crisp, his shoes polished, his weary eyes fixed on her, almost as though he expected her to bolt away at the sight of him.

She certainly considered it, but she knew he'd catch up to her, and she didn't want to make a scene. Instead she pulled back her shoulders and chose the tactic that disarmed many a flustered vendor—meeting him head-on.

"Can I help you?" she asked as she approached.

"We need to talk."

"Follow me." She didn't slow her steps, but walked coolly past him, almost wishing he wouldn't follow her, though she knew him too well to think he'd let her escape now.

"We can talk in my office."

"I'm supposed to meet with the florists at the cathedral in an hour. I need to call them and arrange to meet here, unless you think—"

"You're not leaving the palace grounds today."

"Then I need to call them."

"You can place the call from my office."

Ava did so, drawing out the conversation to avoid talking to Jason, glad he'd closed the door after them so the men in the rooms nearby wouldn't overhear. To her relief, the captain's phone rang just as Ava ran out of advance questions for the florist. She ended the call and couldn't help hearing Jason's conversation.

"Do you have a picture of him—a security-camera

image, anything? Yes, I understand. But tell me, do you know by chance if he was wearing a baseball cap?"

Jason smiled grimly as he ended the call, but when he turned to face Ava, his smile faded, and his grim look turned almost apologetic. "An American, Daniel Johnson, flew into Sardis late Thursday afternoon."

Ava felt her mouth drop open, but she could find no words to speak.

"Given the time of his arrival and the hour when a man arrived at the pedestrian gate, they could well have been the same man. He'd obviously have arrived in time to plant the bomb in your car and drive to your apartment—"

"No!" Ava couldn't listen any longer. "No, he wouldn't do that. He couldn't—how? How did you even learn his name? I didn't tell you."

"Why didn't you?"

"It's not relevant."

"You broke off your engagement suddenly and abandoned your company—"

A horrific sense of betrayal filled Ava. The memory of what Dan had done made Jason's blunt statement even worse. "You went behind my back. Who did you call? Who have you talked to? You should have spoken with me first." Ava planted her hands on Jason's desktop, needing something to lean on as she absorbed this latest blow.

Jason rounded the desk and stood beside her. "Myra told me."

"When did you speak to her?"

"Last evening. I called the number on the brochure—"

"Stop." Ava stood up straight and did her best to stare him down in spite of the six-inch height advantage he held over her. "Don't call anyone else without consulting me first. You've probably upset Myra—"

"I didn't. We had a very pleasant conversation. She wanted me to pass along her greetings and tell you she wishes you every happiness in the world."

Ava pinched her face up tight, trying to hold back the tears. "Sweet Myra. I don't feel guilty about leaving anyone else, but she had a good heart."

"No one else you left had a good heart?" Jason raised an eyebrow. "I need to know about everyone you left behind. You should have told me about Dan Johnson—"

Ava felt as though she'd been punched, and gripped the table again. "Would you please stop saying his name? I don't want to think about any of this."

"I'm sorry, but you have to." Jason kept his voice level, though in the past he'd always raised his volume to match Ava's shouts. "I need to know what happened. If you think there's any legitimate reason at all why D— this person—" Jason refrained from speaking his name at the last moment— "shouldn't be considered a suspect, I would like to know that reason. Considering the circumstances and the timing of his arrival, he's currently my top suspect."

Ava felt her knees giving out under her. She clasped the tabletop desperately, but she felt as though she was being buried under an avalanche of awfulness. First her father, now the man she'd intended to marry? She wished she could forget her engagement had ever happened, but now Jason wanted her to tell him all the horrible details?

Her tears escaped in a flood, and her legs gave out completely at the very same moment. Ava fully expected to land on the floor with a thump, but instead gentle arms lifted her. She leaned on Jason against her better judgment. He perched on the edge of the desk and propped her up beside him, grabbing a handful of tissues from the box near his computer.

"Could Dan have been the man in the security image from the pedestrian gate Thursday night?" Jason asked.

Ava nodded. She didn't even have to think about it. Not only did the man share Dan's build, but he'd stood, spoken and walked like him. "But why would Dan want to kill me? I gave him everything. I walked away."

"This information would make more sense if you'd tell me the whole story." Jason shifted his arm as he spoke, and Ava buried her face against his shoulder. She felt foolish doing so, as though she'd admitted defeat, but what did it matter, really? The man had pulled her, blubbering, from his floor. He'd seen her at her worst and was about to hear her most painful secrets. She might as well find comfort where she could. And Jason had such a perfect shoulder for crying on.

"Dan was my fiancé," she whispered once she'd found her breath. "We'd just become engaged before my mother died. He was my support through all of that. He was all I had, really, besides my business. Then I went to Lydia. When I returned, I found Dan—" Her throat swelled nearly shut.

Jason rubbed her back in that soothing manner she'd come to appreciate.

Ava continued, "He was cheating on me with my business partner, Tiffany. I left them both. I gave Dan back his ring and gave Tiffany Happily Ever After and I came here to stay."

Jason closed his eyes as he held Ava tightly against him and wished he could erase all the awful experiences of her past. So much about the prickly wedding planner made sense now, including the reason why everyone he'd spoken to who'd known her before had called her sweet and kind. She'd changed, hadn't she? Everyone she'd loved had hurt her so deeply she'd retreated inside a hard shell and refused to let anyone in.

Suddenly he realized the precious gift she'd given him, allowing him to witness her brokenness. He wrapped his arms more securely around her. No one was going to hurt her again, not if he had anything to say about it.

Another thought occurred to him. He posed the question as gently as he could. "Was that when you stopped trusting God?"

Ava stiffened and pulled back from him, wiping her eyes with the already-soaked tissues.

Jason pulled out a fresh tissue and wiped her eyes for her. "Ava," he said softly, "I care about you." It wasn't until he'd spoken the words that he realized how much he meant them. He didn't just care about her safety or her relationship with God, although of course he cared about those things.

He cared about *her*.

She met his eyes, and he watched the wariness and the anger war with the temptation to believe him.

"I want to see you smile again," he told her honestly.

Instead of a smile or even the anger he might have expected, Ava's face pinched with sadness. "I don't know how I can ever smile again." She looked him full in the face and admitted, "You're right. That's precisely when I stopped trusting God, and I don't see how I could ever go back, not after all that's happened. If God doesn't love me, why should I love Him? And if God *does* love me, why would He let these awful things happen to me?"

Jason wasn't sure if he should presume to answer, but he cleared his throat anyway. "Do you recall the body I told you I pulled off the island of Dorsi?"

"Yes—the former captain of the guard."

"That's right. He tried to take down the monarchy and nearly ruined the reputation of the royal guard in the process. When all the royals had fled and everything was in shambles and it looked as though evil would win, I asked a very similar question. Where was God? How could He let these things happen to the kingdom of Lydia, which has always been a Christian nation and only ever served Him?"

"Why would God allow all that to happen?" Ava asked adamantly.

"I can't speak for God, but I do know that Lydia is a stronger nation now than we were before. The royal guard is stronger now, though we still have to prove ourselves and earn back our reputation. You wouldn't have any weddings to plan if it hadn't been for the insurgent attacks, because those couples wouldn't have met. Sometimes I think God allows something good to be destroyed so that something better can grow in its place."

Ava closed her eyes as she listened. The sorrow lines eased from her face, and she looked calmer. She opened her eyes and spoke softly. "If I'd kept my business, I wouldn't have relocated here. I enjoy this kingdom and the royal family."

"Is it better than what you had before?"

Ava met his eyes for a long moment. Finally she said softly, "My work is more enjoyable, certainly more prestigious. But the rest of my life?" Her gaze flickered across his face, from his eyes to his lips. Then she turned away. "I'm not sure."

Jason didn't know what to say. He felt attraction stirring inside him, chasing through his veins like a potent drug. Ava had been engaged before she'd left home. Presumably she'd been in love. What would it take for her to find something better here?

He was tempted to pull her back into his arms, to kiss her and insist she was better off with him, but his feelings for her were so new and unfamiliar he didn't dare. She'd been hurt before. If he declared something he wasn't sure of only to discover later he'd been mistaken, he'd hurt her. He didn't want to hurt her, even if he wasn't necessarily in love with her...yet.

Instead he decided to focus on the pressing investigation. Prince Alexander's wedding was a mere week away. They had to catch whoever was after Ava before that event. The safety of everyone attending the wedding was at stake.

"Do you have any pictures of your ex we could circulate? If he's in Lydia, I want to bring him in."

"I can get you pictures." Ava straightened and took another step away from him. "But I have trouble believing it's the same Dan Johnson. That's a common name. It could be just a coincidence. After I broke things off with Dan, he apologized. He sent me flowers. He told me he'd never meant to hurt me, so why would he do something like this?"

"I can't say. The man hurt you once before, and that was a surprise, wasn't it?"

Ava closed her eyes and nodded her head slowly. "I see your point. I'll get you the pictures." She turned toward the door, then glanced back at him. "Do I look all right? I don't want your men to see me—"

Jason grabbed another tissue and gently wiped away a smudge of eye makeup that had crept down her cheek with her tears. "You look beautiful," he said and meant it.

A tiny smile played at her lips, and she sighed. "If someone I once loved is trying to kill me, guess I'd rather it be Dan than my father." She opened the door and exited quickly.

Jason watched her go, still unsure how or why his feelings for her had changed so quickly, or—far more pressing—what he was going to do about it.

Ava no longer had any pictures of Dan, but she was able to go online and find a few decent shots. Rather than email them to Jason, she decided to print them off. Fortunately Jason's men had hooked up her computer and peripherals, and her photo-quality printer quickly spat out the images. Ava checked the time. She had a few extra minutes before her meeting with the florists.

She slid the pictures into a manila envelope. There was time—she could walk them by Jason's office. Email would have been faster, but, she admitted reluctantly to herself, she wanted to see the captain again. Her heart had been so full of emotions when she'd left, and everything between them had changed so quickly. If anything, she wanted to look him full in the face and try to identify what it was she saw there that helped her feel secure in spite of the many threats against her life.

Hurrying up the sidewalk to the royal-guard headquarters building, she stepped through the front door, crossed the foyer to the steel door that led to the hallway to Jason's office, tugged on the door handle and nearly slammed into the door itself when it didn't budge.

"Can I help you?" a voice asked behind her. Was it only her imagination, or was there a hint of amusement underneath the man's words?

Ava turned to the bulletproof-glass panel. Ah, yes, the dispatcher would have to deactivate the lock on the door to let her through. When she'd come through before with Jason, the man must have recognized his captain and let him pass without a word.

"I need to give these to Captain Selini." Ava waved the envelope at the man behind the glass, adding, "He asked for them."

"The captain is in an important meeting right now. I can pass along the envelope to him."

Of course, Ava realized, feeling foolish for assuming she'd be able to monopolize Jason's time. He'd already shoved aside his regular duties to attend to her. She carried the pictures to the window, where a narrow opening at the base provided just enough room for her to slip the envelope through. "Could you ask him to please call me when he gets these? My name is—"

"I know who you are, Ms. Wright." The man behind the tinted glass smiled at her, and Ava realized she'd seen him on various occasions when she visited the royal-guard headquarters, usually to grill the captain on the security details for the weddings and other events she'd planned.

But she didn't know his name, so she simply thanked him and headed back out the front door and across the lawn to the palace for her meeting with the florists, surprised by the disappointment she felt at not being able to see Jason again.

It was silly, of course. She didn't need to see him.

Still, her heart fluttered when her phone rang later, and she saw he was calling her. Her meeting with the florists had just ended, and she was on her way back across the palace lawn toward the palace-wall apartments. She answered the call quickly.

"Do you have a moment this afternoon when you could come by headquarters?"

"I'm free right now." Ava turned around on the sidewalk and headed for the branch that would lead her to the royal-guard building. "If it's not too soon."

"The sooner the better."

To Ava's relief, this time when she entered the foyer, Jason was there to meet her.

"Do you have your schedule for the coming week with you?" He held open the door to the hallway.

"Of course." She stepped through, then waited for Jason, unsure where they were headed.

He stopped in his office first as she called up the full-week overview on her tablet.

"It seems you're only truly safe when you're inside the palace walls," Jason observed. "I'd like to keep you here at all times. How difficult will that be?"

"I can change the location of most of my meetings so that I don't have to leave the palace grounds." Ava looked over her schedule as she spoke, checking for anything that might require her to leave. "Of course, next Friday I'll have to go in person to the Sardis Cathedral for the final check of the wedding decor, and then the rehearsal. And Saturday is the wedding itself."

"If there's anything you need before then, we can send a palace staff member to get it for you. Under no circumstances do I want you leaving without a full guard detail."

"Full detail?" Ava clarified.

"At least three guards. If you have more people with you, the proportion of guards will change, but I don't want to take any chances."

Ava swallowed. She knew she ought to feel protected, but instead his words made her feel threatened. "Your guards don't like me," she reminded him.

"That's not my fault." His expression, which up until that moment had been compassionate, now hardened.

"Isn't it?" she challenged him. After all, he was the only member of the guard she'd worked closely with. It seemed to her his men had picked up on his attitude.

"Ava," he snapped, "I'm trying to help you."

Ava stared at Jason as she debated how to respond to his claim. Should she apologize or stand her ground? Her words had been completely honest, so she saw no reason to take them back. She didn't want his men anywhere near her, but at the same time, she knew the threat against her life was real. And though she couldn't deny her increasing affection toward Jason, her instincts told her to push him away before she was hurt any worse.

But before she could make up her mind to say anything, Jason spoke again. "As long as you're not planning to leave the palace grounds before Friday, it won't be an issue. I've circulated the photographs you passed along to me. Hopefully, we won't have anything to worry about by Friday."

"Good." Ava put her schedule away and turned toward the door. She glanced back for just a moment, unsure if she should thank him or fight with him or give in to what she really wanted and throw herself into his arms.

Jason nodded curtly.

Ava nodded back and left in silence. She wasn't sure what they had going on between them. They could either be enemies or something quite the opposite, but Ava had far too much going on to allow herself the indulgence of wasting time trying to sort out whatever it was between her and the captain.

Until they caught whoever was trying to kill her, she didn't figure there was any way she'd be able to examine the question with a clear head anyway.

ELEVEN

By Tuesday, Jason was ready to pull his hair out in frustration. They had no new leads, no new developments, no sign of the American Daniel Johnson, and each day when Jason called the church in Seattle, a different secretary told him Ava's father wasn't there. None of them would tell him where the pastor was or how Jason might reach him. The royal-wedding date was quickly approaching, and with it, the certainty that Ava would have to leave the safety of the palace walls.

Most frustrating of all, Ava had turned cold toward him again. Or perhaps *cold* wasn't quite the word. She hadn't gone back to her argumentative ways completely, but she watched him warily, as though unsure whether he could be trusted.

As if Jason didn't have enough on his mind, he found himself constantly stewing over just what was going on between him and Ava. They had a distinct chemistry between them, he knew that much. It had always been there, he realized now, but for the longest time they'd merely screamed at each other because of it. He didn't want to argue with her anymore. Somehow he had to convince the hurt girl under the armor that it was safe to lower her defenses.

But as long as a killer was after her, it wouldn't be safe for her to lower her defenses, not really.

When Jason's phone rang in the early afternoon on Tuesday, he recognized her number and answered quickly, though at that moment he stood in front of a roomful of transfers from the Lydian army, explaining to them in detail the differences between life in the army and life in the royal guard.

"I have an hour," Ava said without preamble. "Can I meet with you?"

"Right now?" Jason had one foot up on the table, demonstrating a proper shoe-polish shine to the new recruits.

"This is the only block of time I have free before ten o'clock tonight. It's rather urgent."

Jason couldn't help wondering what qualified as urgent. Had she learned something new, recalled an old, forgotten death threat? He couldn't put off meeting with her, not if it meant a possible break in the case. "I'll meet you in the foyer." He dismissed the men, instructing them to return promptly in one hour.

Ava didn't speak until Jason closed his office door after her. Then she met his eyes and said bluntly, "I can't do this."

For one light-headed instant, Jason thought perhaps she was going to confess her feelings for him, reach across the desk and kiss him. But she glared at him rigidly from the other side of his desk, so clearly a kiss was the furthest thing from her mind.

"I cannot in good conscience appear at the royal wedding and endanger the lives of everyone there."

He held his breath, fearing she'd announce she was leaving.

Ava pinched her face into a pain-filled expression that

was by now all too familiar to him. She added, "Nor can I leave on such short notice."

Relieved that her stubborn mind wasn't set on going, Jason nonetheless couldn't see what she was getting at. "What other choice is there?" He'd toyed with the idea of using technology to allow her to supervise the wedding from a remote location, but the technical difficulties that presented—combined with the thick stone walls of the cathedral, which were notorious for deflecting transmitted signals of every sort—had forced him to dismiss that possibility without ever suggesting it.

"I can't keep hiding from the inevitable. If I wait until the day before the wedding to show my face, there's sure to be an incident, and any member of the royal family might be hurt."

"You're not thinking—"

But Ava cut him off, slapping down a sheaf of papers with articles she'd printed out. "I've done research on assassination attempts. Did you know that in 1842, when Queen Victoria of England was riding in her carriage, a man stepped out and aimed a pistol at her? He tried to shoot her, but his gun didn't go off."

"I'm familiar with that story." As head of royal security in Lydia, Jason had made it a point to familiarize himself with the major historical incidents involving royal safety. "Didn't they catch him the very next day?"

"Yes. The queen rode her carriage along the same route at the same time, but this time she had plainclothes police positioned to catch him. When the man stepped out to try it again, he was captured."

"That was a long time ago. Guns don't often fail to go off anymore. The world was a different place then," Jason cautioned Ava. He could guess what she was getting at, and wanted to slow her momentum before she became too caught up in her plan.

"It's not that different. We could lure him out."

"No."

"I've thought about this a great deal, Jason. It could work."

"You can't go out there as bait."

"What's the alternative? I stay inside the palace forever?"

"Not forever. Just until…"

"Until when?"

"Until whoever is after you gives up and goes home."

"How do you know that hasn't already happened?"

Jason had expected a sharp retort, but Ava's choice of words surprised him. "How— What?"

"Nothing has happened in the last three days. Maybe I'm safe already and we just don't know it. For all you know, I could leave the palace and be fine."

"And then what? You'd go on with your life without a full guard detail? I don't think so."

Ava glared at him for a long stretch of silence. He could see her weighing her options, choosing her words. "I'll make you a deal."

Jason raked his hand back through his hair. "What kind of deal?"

"Let's try luring him out. You pick the time, the place, the number of guards. If anyone attempts to attack me, we'll capture him. And if not—" she took a step closer and met his eyes without blinking "—I'll let you assign me a full guard detail for as long as you deem it necessary."

Jason blew out a breath he hadn't realized he'd been holding back. Ava had a knack for making deals he couldn't refuse. He'd prayed for a way to convince her to accept the full guard detail. She'd walked into his office and proposed it herself.

He couldn't turn down such an obvious answer to prayer, even if it meant risking the safety of the woman he'd come to care about so much. "Fine."

"Yes?"

"Yes, fine, we'll do it."

Ava grinned at him and stepped forward, right arm extended.

Jason reached for her, ready to hug her, then fumbled awkwardly when it appeared she only meant to shake his hand. He recovered, shaking her hand solidly as he told her, "I pick the time and the place? You'll clear your schedule?"

"I'll do whatever needs to be done. This will work. It has to."

"Does it?" Jason had his doubts that her plan would succeed, and couldn't imagine the source of her confidence.

But her smile faded quickly and she cast him a sober look. "I don't know what we'll do if it doesn't."

Finally understanding her meaning, Jason wished she'd hugged him. Instead she turned and left. He couldn't help wondering if he'd have another opportunity to hold her. If her plan failed...well, Ava was right about one thing. Her plan had better work.

Jason spent the rest of his hour working out the details. Given the quickly approaching wedding, it made sense for Ava to go on her outing as soon as possible. She'd told him she was booked until ten that evening, but she'd also promised to clear her schedule for him. He wanted as many men as he could get on hand to protect Ava and apprehend anyone who might try to harm her. And since he was eager to proceed before his better judgment prevailed, the only time that made sense was the evening shift change.

A quick call to Ava confirmed she'd move her appointments to make the time work. When Jason's men filed in at the end of the hour, shoes shining, Jason quickly enlisted their support.

"Do any of you have a problem with working an hour later than usual tonight?" To his relief, none of the men had pressing plans. Jason proceeded to fill them in on the details, but when he mentioned Ava's name, the men didn't try very hard to muffle their snickers.

Jason stopped midsentence and glared at them. "Is there a problem?"

"Are you sure you want us to protect her?" Titus asked.

"It might be a convenient way to—" Adrian started.

Jason didn't let him finish. "Let's get one thing straight right now. Yes, Ava and I have argued in the past. Yes, she can be headstrong and demanding, but she is every bit as deserving of your respect as any other member of the royal household. I will not tolerate any hint of disrespect toward her in the future. Is that clear?"

His men looked first surprised and then chastened.

Taking advantage of their silence, Jason added, "This is what I've been trying to impress upon you about the difference between the royal guard and the army. Honor goes both ways. If you want people to respect you and the uniform you wear, you must respect all those you protect." Jason looked his men in the eye each in turn as they absorbed his words. He could have said more. In fact, his thoughts spun with examples of Ava's attributes—her selfless concern for others, her grace under trial, her persistence—but he didn't trust himself to say any more, not without revealing the depth of his feelings for the woman.

The men listened silently and respectfully as Jason outlined the rest of the plan. After a few clarifying questions, they filed out to prepare for their mission by changing into civilian clothes and choosing their positions along the route between the palace and the marina. Since he and Ava had been followed to Dorsi, Jason could only assume her would-be killer would be watching the same route. Of course, there was every chance the man might miss them as they passed by, even if he was still out to kill her. Even if nothing happened today, he wouldn't reconsider whether her life was really in danger. Until Dan—or whoever was trying to kill her—was caught, Ava was in danger.

All the more reason why Jason wanted to see Ava's plan through quickly—so he could assign a full guard detail to her without any further objection.

As planned, Ava exited the palace promptly at six and approached the garages from across the courtyard. Jason watched her walk toward him, her posture as authoritative as ever, her navy slacks and coordinating blue-and-white top crisp in spite of the long day already behind her. And yet, in spite of her uptilted chin, Jason could see the shadow of fear that haunted her eyes, the slight uncertainty as she glanced toward the remaining guards who hadn't yet taken positions on the route ahead of them.

Then her eyes landed on him and her face immediately relaxed. She didn't smile, necessarily, but she certainly looked relieved and possibly even glad to see him.

Jason grinned at her as she came to a stop next to him. "Ready to take a walk?"

She nodded. "Ready as I'll ever be."

Jason signaled a pair of men to fall out ahead of them. "We'll follow in a moment," he explained to Ava, "and the last men will trail us at a distance. I have guards positioned at regular intervals between the palace and the marina."

Ava fell into step beside him and they walked through the pedestrian gate in silence.

"Perhaps we should chat," Jason suggested after signaling the last of his men to follow them. "We need to act natural."

"Good idea—but let's talk about something other than what we're doing right now. I'd like to get my mind off all of this."

"Yes, that's smart," Jason agreed, thinking. "How was your day?"

"I don't want to discuss that, either." A distressed note ran through Ava's voice.

The situation was getting to her. Jason needed to calm her down or cheer her up, and he needed to do it quickly. If the would-be killer sensed a trap, their jaunt to the marina might do more harm than good.

It had been years since Jason had been the class clown. He hadn't thought about his old jokes in years, and tried to recall what he used to do that had been so funny. "When I was younger I wanted to be a ventriloquist."

Ava looked completely taken aback by his announcement. "You did? Seriously?"

"Yes. My family had a pet parrot named Pepe, but he couldn't speak. He would sit on my shoulder, and I'd go around trying to convince everyone Pepe could talk."

"You talked for the parrot?"

Jason nodded, he memories returning. "The best part was I could get away with saying things I normally couldn't. There was a fish stall down the street from our house. The fisherman was stingy and didn't like tourists. He tried to take advantage of them by selling them old fish, so my parrot would warn them."

"What? How?" Ava walked more slowly, watching Jason as they ambled down the street.

Putting on his best parrot voice, Jason imitated the bird, "This fish stinks! It's old, it's old," he squawked, adding quickly in his own voice, "Pepe, that's rude. You shouldn't talk like that." And then squawking, "He shouldn't sell old fish!"

Whether it was the bird's voice coming out of the captain's mouth or simply her nerves getting the best of her, Ava laughed—not just a giggle or a smile, but full-out laughter.

Encouraged, Jason added with Pepe's signature squawk, "Don't touch the fish! It stinks! It stinks!"

To his surprise, Ava not only continued to laugh, but she clutched her stomach and threw her head back, stopping still on the street.

Jason stopped, too, beaming as he watched her. It felt good to make someone laugh again, but far more than that, his heart soared at the sight of Ava laughing.

Once she'd caught her breath enough to speak, Ava said, "I can't imagine you got away with that routine many times."

"Pepe was eventually banned from the fish stall, but not before some tourists tipped off the Food Safety Board. They nearly shut his stall down, but he cleaned up his act."

"So it all ended well." Ava's smile lingered, brightening her face and chasing the fear to the far corners of her eyes.

"Yes." Jason gazed at her a moment longer, amazed

by the way her smile transformed her face, revealing her true beauty. Then he cleared his throat. "We should keep going."

"We should," Ava said, glancing about them nervously, fear flooding her features once again.

So Jason added in Pepe's voice, "We should keep going."

"I can't if you keep making me laugh like that," Ava said, swatting at his arm.

Jason screeched quietly, "Assault! Assault!"

Ava recovered from her laughter enough to ask, "How do you do that without moving your mouth?"

They paused on the cobbled street again. Jason knew they weren't going to reach the marina very quickly at this rate, but he figured the point of the plan was for Ava to be visible. The longer it took them to reach their destination, the more visible they'd be.

Jason demonstrated in Pepe's voice, "You've got to open your mouth just a small amount, but hold your lips still, like this."

"Like this?" Ava tried, but she burst out laughing again and ruined whatever might have come of her attempt.

"More like this. Use your teeth instead of your lips."

"Ny theeth?" Ava mangled the words. "Like thith?"

However much he might have wanted to assist her, Jason couldn't help chuckling at the sight of the usually stern-faced wedding planner attempting to speak without moving her lips. Besides that, he was glad for the excuse to laugh. He hadn't realized before how lovely her lips were, how perfectly they framed her teeth or how she glowed when she laughed. The formidable wedding planner was transformed when she smiled, and he felt his attitude toward her changing just as quickly as the expression on her face.

Getting in on the act, Ava added, "Thith could come in handy at wedding rehearthalth."

At the thought of Ava attempting the act in front of a nervous wedding party, Jason couldn't help laughing even harder. It was that or give in to the temptation to explore how her lips felt against his.

That was beyond consideration.

So why couldn't he stop thinking about it?

Ava blushed, giggling.

As he wiped the tears of laughter from his eyes, watching Ava giggle self-consciously, Jason couldn't help wondering if he'd finally found the real Ava, underneath all her armor and sternness. He sincerely hoped so, because he was falling in love with this woman, whoever she was. He could only pray this Ava would supplant the stern-faced wedding planner, because he didn't want to lose this woman.

TWELVE

Gratitude surged through Ava's heart as she laughed at the uncharacteristically playful captain. She couldn't recall when she'd last laughed—really laughed—with her head thrown back, clutching her sides as though she might burst. She certainly hadn't expected to laugh today, but Jason had somehow accomplished the impossible.

She'd so needed the break from the constant fear and stress. "You're far more fun to laugh with than to argue with," she confessed as they started walking toward the marina again.

"Oh? I thought you rather enjoyed arguing with me." The captain's tone was still playful, not accusatory.

Ava answered honestly, "Actually, I rather have enjoyed arguing with you. Is that an awful thing for me to say? You fight fair. You follow my reasoning, and you stick to your principles. I hope I haven't been too much of a pain."

"I'm glad you feel that way about our arguments," Jason said, surprising her. "You'll probably want to argue with me again about the wedding plans. If we don't catch anyone today, I'm going to ask you to reconsider your plan for Prince Alexander and Lillian to travel from the cathedral back to the palace in an open carriage."

His words chased away her laughter.

Though she shared Jason's concerns for the royal couple's safety, Ava always promised her brides the wedding of their dreams. She couldn't go back on their promise now, certainly not because of a problem that only existed because of her. "Lillian specifically requested a horse-drawn carriage. She loves horses. She'd have arrived on a horse if I hadn't convinced her it wouldn't work with the dress she'd chosen. The carriage was our compromise."

"I appreciate that," Jason acknowledged, "but safety is more important than having the wedding of one's dreams. If you'd like, I can meet with the couple and explain—"

"Please don't—not without me. It's all my fault. All week long I've been inconveniencing everyone to meet at the palace. We've got to capture whoever's after me."

Jason cast a meaningful glance toward the marina. They were almost there, and they hadn't seen or heard the slightest hint of trouble. "I'm afraid we're not doing very well at that."

Having thought over her plan for some time before she'd even approached Jason to suggest it, Ava had already considered one possible scenario that now seemed even more likely. Unwilling to speak the words very loudly, she leaned close to Jason and whispered, "What if he's out there watching us right now, but he's made a plan to strike during the wedding on Saturday, so he's not acting now? He's purposely waiting."

The captain made a discontented rumbling noise in his throat. Ava wished he'd deny her suggestion, in Pepe's voice if necessary, but instead he said, "That's a distinct possibility, but I hope it's not the case."

"I hope not, either." Her lighthearted laughter now completely doused by fear, Ava shivered.

They finished their walk in silence, reaching the marina and continuing on down the dock toward the spot where the royal-guard speedboat was moored. They stopped beside the boat.

Ava looked up at Jason. "Now what?"

"We walk back to the palace."

"Isn't that admitting defeat?"

"You have appointments this evening, don't you?"

"I cleared the hour. We've only been walking for ten minutes." Ava felt desperation rising within her. The gunman needed to show himself again. Whoever was after her had to show up. The plea rose inside her, almost like a prayer. In times past she would have prayed, before she'd learned God didn't answer and didn't care. And yet where else did she have to turn?

"Ava! Ava!"

She heard her name, shouted from some distance, and turned to see a man in a baseball cap running toward her.

Jason's men were on him in an instant, but even more quickly, Jason tucked Ava against him, holding her tight to the protective shell of his body armor. She clung to him for a long moment as she listened to the sounds of the guards and tried to figure out what was happening. She wished she was close enough to see the man or hear his voice clearly. Was she in danger? Was Jason in danger, shielding her from the man who'd run at them?

Terror clenched the air from her lungs. What if something happened to Jason? What if he was hurt protecting her? She buried her face against his shoulder and listened to the reassuring beat of his heart thumping solidly beneath her cheek.

Jason had done so much for her already. He made her

feel safe. He made her feel happy. He made her feel…
things she hadn't been willing to feel for so long. She
couldn't lose him now, not when she'd only just begun
to realize how much he meant to her.

Not when she had yet to tell him what he meant to her.

Jason conferred with his men via his earpiece, in-
structing them to escort the suspect up to headquarters.
He straightened slowly, keeping one arm tight around
Ava's shoulders, supporting her as she stood.

Perhaps she should let go and put some space between them, but Ava didn't want to let go of Jason. She
needed his strength to remain upright. She felt far too
shaky to stand alone as she absorbed the shock of what
had happened.

They'd caught him. She was nearly certain, from the
brief glimpse she'd seen, that the man who'd run down the
pier after her was Dan Johnson, her former fiancé. And
everything from his Mariners cap to his stature appeared
to be identical to what she'd viewed on the security-camera
footage of the man who'd inquired after her at the pedestrian gate five days before.

She'd feared Dan might be the culprit. His identity
wasn't nearly as shocking as his timing. After refusing
to pray for so many months, a wordless, half-suppressed
prayer had welled up inside her heart just before she'd
heard Dan calling her name.

It made her wonder if God was trying to tell her something. But if that was the case, why had God waited until
now, when she'd pleaded for answers so many months
before?

While his men detained the suspect, Jason conferred
with Ava in his office. "You have appointments—"

"Not for another half hour. If you question him now, I can hear what he has to say."

"It may well take more than half an hour."

"Then I'll clear my schedule—"

"You've already done that so much—"

"It doesn't matter, not in comparison to finding out what's been going on."

"We always tape suspect interviews. You can watch it later."

"How am I supposed to focus on final dress fittings when I know you're interviewing Dan at the same moment? We're wasting time. Let me listen now. If it takes longer than half an hour, I'll go to the dress fitting and come back to watch the tape when I'm done."

Jason listened to Ava's proposal reluctantly. He didn't want her anywhere near that dangerous man, but he supposed that was his heart trying to tell his head what to do. And if he listened to his heart, he'd have Ava back in his arms in an instant. No, better to think with his head, not his emotions. Her idea was a good one. "Fine. Let's get started."

Escorting Ava to the small room behind the one-way glass, Jason assured her she wouldn't be seen from the other side as long as the lights remained off on her side of the glass. "It will look like a mirror from the other side. There's a curtain in front of the door, so if anyone enters, the light from the hallway won't shine in." Jason pulled the curtain closed as he explained it. "Are you sure—"

"Yes. Get on with it. I'll be fine."

Jason left quickly, entering the adjoining room and instructing his men to bring in the suspect for questioning.

Though he couldn't see her through the mirrored glass, from the last glimpse he'd gotten of her before leaving her alone, he didn't think Ava looked nearly as okay as she claimed to be. She looked as if she needed to be in his arms, and he wanted her there, but none of that could happen just yet. Besides, he needed to keep a lid on his newfound feelings. His men had already raised their eyebrows after the way Jason had held her on the pier and laughed with her along their walk.

He figured they suspected something. They were trained to read body language. He wouldn't be able to keep his secret for long, though it chafed him to think of admitting there was anything between him and the wedding planner before he'd had a chance to speak to Ava about his feelings. Besides that, he'd specifically instructed his men on several past occasions not to romance the women they were guarding.

How would they like it if he did the very thing he'd ordered them not to do?

Dan Johnson entered between two guards, glancing at Jason only briefly before looking around the room.

"I need to talk to Ava Wright," Dan told Jason bluntly, refusing to be seated when the guards gestured for him to sit.

"Have a seat. You're going to talk to me first. If I decide Ms. Wright needs to hear what you have to say, I'll pass the message along to her."

The man sat but leaned toward Jason. "It's a matter of life and death. I know that sounds melodramatic, but that's just the way it is."

Jason had enough experience interrogating suspects not to let the man control the conversation or distract him from his work. Ava had less than half an hour to listen—he wouldn't waste her time. "State your full name."

But Dan didn't cooperate. "Someone blew up Ava's car the other day, didn't they? And something must have spooked you guys, because you moved her out of her apartment. I watched your men do it. You know she's in danger, don't you?"

Normally Jason would have interrupted the man and insisted Dan answer the questions posed to him, but something about the man's words—his persistence, his knowledge of the situation—was enough to prompt Jason to listen. The guards had moved Ava's things from her apartment while Jason and Ava had been at Dorsi, being chased by the gunman.

Was Dan trying to create an alibi? Or had he really been watching the movers at work? But if he hadn't been on the island, who had been? The gunman had been wearing a cap identical to the one Dan wore now.

Even as Jason wondered about it, Dan continued, "I believe someone's trying to hurt Ava—"

"From what I understand," Jason interrupted, unable to let the man play altruistic after what he'd done to Ava, "you hurt her."

Dan pinched his eyes shut and made a frustrated noise in his throat. When he popped his eyes open again, he spoke quickly. "Yes, I did, but now that I know what I know, I see it wasn't really my fault at all."

"You cheated on her with her best friend and business partner." Jason had learned through previous interrogation attempts that it was sometimes useful to surprise a suspect with the facts he knew. It might startle the suspect into revealing something he otherwise wouldn't, and it helped if he needed to pretend to know more than he really did.

"Tiffany seduced me," Dan countered without blinking. "And then, once it was clear Ava had left and wasn't coming back, Tiffany dropped me suddenly and for no reason. It didn't make sense. It was as though she'd only used me to hurt Ava."

"Why would she do that?"

"Yes, why?" Dan narrowed his eyes. "I puzzled it over for a long time before I heard Happily Ever After was struggling to stay in business. I couldn't understand. They'd been so successful when Ava led the company. I decided I wanted answers. I paid Tiffany a visit."

Jason listened intently, wondering if the man's words were true or just a carefully concocted cover story meant to conceal Dan's guilt. Unsure, he let the man continue his story and hoped he'd learn something definitive soon. It couldn't be easy for Ava, sitting alone on the other side of the mirror, to hear Dan's words—especially the sudden revelation that the business she'd poured her heart into was floundering without her.

"Tiffany gave me all sorts of reasons and excuses, but the thing I found most disturbing was that she tried to blame all her failures on Ava. She resents Ava—deeply. It sounded like she's been jealous of Ava's success for a long time and only pretended to be her friend while she leeched off her and tried to bring her down. Tiffany admitted the company was going under, but claimed it was Ava's fault, that she'd only given her the company after she'd realized it would fail, that Ava had left Tiffany in charge on purpose to make it look like the failure was Tiffany's fault. But from everything I know of the company, it didn't begin to fail until these last several months since Tiffany's been in charge."

Dan shook his head and swallowed before he continued, "I decided to investigate. My excuse for visiting Tiffany was that she still had my golf clubs. We went to her garage to get them. She has a two-car garage. There were two vehicles inside—the one she used to have and the one she bought shortly before Ava left for Lydia. Her old car looked as though it had been in a fender bender. The front was smashed in a bit and a small chunk was missing. I asked her what happened and she told me she'd hit a mailbox. Then I asked why she hadn't gotten it fixed."

Jason raised an eyebrow when Dan hesitated.

"She said she didn't want anyone asking questions."

"Questions?" Jason repeated. If Dan was making up his story, he'd rehearsed it well ahead of time, well enough to make his body language fit the true discomfort of a man who'd discovered more than he'd ever wanted to know.

"The thing is—" Dan leaned close "—the piece that was missing was a silver chunk, an odd shape, sort of like a triangle with a bulge at the base. But when Ava's mother was killed in a hit-and-run accident, they found a silver triangle like that missing piece in the street in front of her house. They couldn't say for sure if it had come from the car that hit her, but they circulated a picture of it next to a dollar bill for size. I saw it dozens of times." Dan sat back and eyed him with finality. "It matched."

"Did you call the police?"

"I did, the very next day. In retrospect I should have called sooner, but I didn't make the connection until that evening, and then it took me all night to get over my denial and place the call. By the time the police arrived, the car was gone and so was Tiffany."

"Tiffany was gone?"

Dan nodded solemnly.

"When was this?"

"Sunday of last week—nine days ago now. I puzzled over everything for another day and couldn't shake a few things Tiffany had said about Ava, bitter things, threatening things. And I realized that if Tiffany killed Ava's mom—which I fear she may have—then the threatening things she said about Ava weren't just old bitterness. They were real."

Jason didn't like what he was hearing. He especially didn't like thinking about Ava hearing it all from behind the glass, but he had to find answers. Dan's story seemed convincing, but it could still well just be a story. "I trust you called the police again."

"Yes, of course. They sent someone to talk to Tiffany, but she still wasn't home. What else could they do? From their perspective, I'd given them two dead-end tips. The car wasn't there. Tiffany wasn't there. I realized if Tiffany was out to hurt Ava, she might have traveled to Lydia. I talked to her secretary, Myra, who was trying to hold the company together. At first she told me she wasn't supposed to tell anyone where Tiffany had gone. When I guessed Lydia, she confirmed it."

"Tiffany is in Lydia?" Jason clarified, starting to believe the man's story might be true and fearing the implications if it was.

"Myra booked the tickets herself."

"*Tickets?* More than one?"

"Myra wouldn't tell me the name of the man who was traveling with Tiffany. I only know it's a man because Myra referred to him as 'he.' I called Ava's father. He refused to give me her contact information or even listen to what I had to say. I can't really blame him, not after I cheated on his daughter."

Dan's introspective pause and honest words convinced Jason the man might actually be telling the truth. He couldn't prove anything just yet, but he was willing to pursue any tips the man might give him.

At the same time, Jason wasn't about to turn the man loose based on a story. The gunman on the island had been wearing a Seattle Mariners baseball cap identical to the one Dan wore at that very moment. Ava had suggested the gunman might have chosen the cap to throw them off the trail, but Jason wasn't about to deny that Dan matched everything they knew about the gunman, save for his story—which could be an elaborately concocted alibi.

"I've sent him several emails explaining what I think is going on. I've left messages on his phone. He won't answer my calls. Look…" Dan met his eyes, and Jason thought he saw real regret there. "I wish I could take back what I did. Ava was the sweetest, most wonderful woman I ever could have hoped for, but I blew it. I can't go back in time and change what I did, but I wish I could. When I realized Tiffany had come here after Ava, and I couldn't convince anyone to stop her, I knew that I had to come, or I'd spend the rest of my life regretting that I didn't save her when I had the chance."

Jason asked, "Did you inquire after her at the palace gate last Thursday evening?"

"Yes. I didn't have her phone number. She changed her email address. I had no way of getting in touch with her. I've tried everything. When I couldn't find Ava, I tried to track down Tiffany. I knew I couldn't give up. I saw Ava this evening and just started running toward her, calling her name. And now here I am."

A quick glance at the clock told Jason that Ava only had a few minutes left before she needed to leave. After what they'd both just heard, he couldn't let her go before speaking with her, nor did he want to make her late. Quickly instructing his men to detain Dan for further questioning, he excused himself to slip into the small adjoining room, praying he could offer Ava some comfort.

Had Tiffany really killed Ava's mother? It certainly

seemed possible—unless Dan Johnson was lying. But Dan would surely only have lied to cover his own guilt, which meant Dan might have been the murderer besides trying to kill Ava. Either way, someone Ava had once trusted and cared about had done the unthinkable...and seemed intent on killing Ava, as well.

THIRTEEN

Ava gripped her chair and stared through the glass, too stunned to move a muscle. A thousand thoughts warred inside her head. Was Dan telling the truth? Had Tiffany killed her mother? And what had she ever seen in Dan anyway? He was good-looking enough and usually well dressed, but those were all his good points.

He couldn't compare to Jason. Where Dan had been hesitant, unsure and even whiny, Jason was commanding yet caring, a man of action who stood by his principles. And Jason had a much nicer smile than Dan. The thought of Jason made Ava wish she was still tucked under his protective arm, clinging tightly to him as she had done on the pier.

She watched through the glass as Jason left the interrogation room. As he joined her, she rose from her chair, but instantly she felt light-headed from standing so quickly after sitting frozen through such shocking revelations.

Jason pulled her into his arms and she held tight to him, leaning on him for support. The comfort of his touch loosened her frozen lungs. She could breathe again and pulled in a lungful of his manly scent, grateful for his presence. Ever since he'd held her on the pier, she'd longed to feel his arms around her again. No one was shooting at her at the moment, so she wasn't sure why Jason had pulled her into his arms.

Was it because he knew she needed his strength to stand? Did she look that unstable? Or did he really care about her that much? It didn't make sense that he would—not after all the nasty arguments between them. And yet Jason held her close and even lightly rubbed her back, his touch soothing and reassuring.

"What do you think?" he asked after rubbing her back a moment.

Ava's thoughts swam, but she picked one memory that stuck out like a red flag now that Dan's story shone a light on it. "Tiffany missed several important appointments. I always covered for her. My mother found out about it and advised me to make Tiffany face the consequences of her own decisions. Tiffany walked in on our conversation." Ava swallowed, her throat thick. "That wasn't long before my mother died. I don't remember how long exactly, but…it makes sense."

"Dan's story makes sense?"

"I don't like it. I wish I could say Dan was the gunman, lock him up and I'll be safe, everyone at the wedding will be safe." Her voice rose to an emotional whimper. She wondered if she was rambling.

"His story makes sense to me, too," Jason admitted, still rubbing her back. "At the same time, he's wearing the same hat as the gunman who followed us to Dorsi. They have the same build. It could just be an elaborate story he's telling us. He could be the gunman."

"I can't believe I was ever in love with him."

"He seems like a nice guy. If his story is true, he did the right thing by coming here to warn you."

"I do appreciate that—if his story is true." Ava peeled

back a bit from Jason, knowing she needed to leave. "Still, he's nothing like you."

"Nothing like me?" Jason asked quietly.

Realizing that she'd revealed more of her feelings than she'd intended, Ava blushed and tried to explain. "He's not decisive and principled and strong like you are." She met Jason's eyes and saw him watching her with a hint of a smile.

And she realized her explanation had revealed even more of her feelings, instead of disguising them. Embarrassed though she was, Ava wouldn't deny that she'd come to trust and care for Jason so much it frightened her.

She had to retreat. "I need to get going."

"I have feelings for you," Jason said quietly as Ava stepped past him.

She turned and looked him full in the face. "Hmm?"

"All those times we argued, it wasn't because I was mad at you. It was because I found you maddening."

"Those aren't the same thing?" Ava's heart swelled. What kind of feelings did Jason have for her? Was he simply being kind to her because he felt sorry she'd had to endure so much? Or did he care for her as more than a friend?

"This is probably horrible timing," Jason confessed, taking her hand, "but you said what you said and I wanted you to know your feelings are precious to me. I wake up thinking of you. My day doesn't really start until I see your face. And when you laughed earlier? I was king of the world. I'd love to make you laugh again."

Ava drew closer to Jason as he spoke. She couldn't believe she was hearing such kind words from a man who'd spoken to her so sharply just the week before. As he mentioned her laugh, he brushed her cheek gently with one hand. Ava rose on tiptoes, pulling closer to him, yearning for his touch after sitting alone through the awful interview.

Jason leaned down toward her. She realized a moment before his lips touched hers that he might very well be going to kiss her. Then he hesitated and she feared he might change his mind, so she closed the distance between them just as he did the same, and their lips met with urgency.

She'd enjoyed arguing with Jason. She'd enjoyed laughing with him even more. But neither of those things nor both together could compare with kissing him. If there had been any doubt in her mind that Jason was a better fit for her than Dan ever could have been, the kiss confirmed it.

She didn't want to ever stop kissing him. So what if she was late for the dress fitting? The dressmakers could assess the bridesmaids without her. It wasn't as though she had to be there.

Eyes closed tight, her whole self focused on the feel and the smell and the taste of this wonderful man, Ava vaguely realized Jason had cleared his throat.

It wasn't until she heard the sound again that she realized Jason couldn't possibly have made the noise, as he was still ardently kissing her.

"Um, Captain?"

That was most definitely not Jason's voice.

Ava opened her eyes and discovered two men standing in the doorway.

And they'd pulled the curtain back and turned the light on. The one-way glass had become two-way glass, and a room full of royal guards had witnessed their kiss.

Mortified, Ava took a second to recover. "I need to be

going." She slipped from Jason's arms, retreating quickly down the hall and toward the palace.

What had she done? She'd kissed the captain of the guard. That had been lovely. But all his men had witnessed it. Grateful as she was that she'd gotten away quickly, she couldn't help feeling a bit guilty for leaving Jason alone to face his men. No matter what he chose to talk about, it was certain to be an awkward conversation.

Jason watched Ava walk away. Then he looked at his men and cleared his throat. "Inform Mr. Johnson we'll be looking into his story, but in the meantime, we're going to keep him here under guard. Or I can tell him myself." Jason started to step past the men, who seemed frozen in place, unsure how to react to what they'd seen.

Titus cleared his throat. "Captain, you've got a bit of pink—" he gestured around his own mouth "—lipstick?"

A couple of guards stifled giggles.

But Linus and Galen, two guards who'd witnessed the kiss from the other side of the glass, didn't look at all amused. Jason had warned each of them not to become involved with the women they were guarding. And though Linus was now engaged to Duchess Julia, and Galen was likewise engaged to Ruby Tate, Princess Anastasia's assistant, Jason had discouraged those romances. He'd even gone so far as to threaten Galen that he'd lose his job if he became involved with Ruby.

Jason owed his men an explanation. It wasn't a conversation he wanted to have, but he figured he wouldn't gain anything by putting it off.

"Titus, pass the message along to the suspect and detain him in cell B. Then join me in the conference room. I need to address everyone together."

Stepping into the nearby men's room, Jason checked

his reflection in the mirror and wiped the lipstick away. What had he done? What would he tell the men? He needed to talk to Ava about what was going on between them, but there wasn't time for that. His men deserved answers. Now—before any of them had an opportunity to grumble.

The men were still waiting for him in the conference room. He gathered his thoughts as he faced them.

"We talk a lot about honor in the royal guard," he began. "It's been my goal to restore the reputation of the guard, to restore our honor." Jason swallowed, trying to think how his behavior fit his words. "The Royal Guard Code of Honor specifically prohibits improper behavior between guards and those they protect."

Months before, Jason had looked up the exact clause to guide him as he responded to the relationships blossoming between his guards and those they guarded. He still hadn't made up his mind precisely what those centuries-old words meant.

Clearly his guards struggled with the same confusion. Galen asked quietly, "What is improper behavior?"

Jason looked at him and tried to think of an answer.

Linus spoke first. "Was that kiss proper behavior?"

"I don't know," Jason admitted. "What do you men think?"

By that time, Titus had returned along with several more guards. The large conference room was getting crowded.

"Do you know what I think?" Royal guard Levi Grenaldo, recently married to Princess Isabelle, spoke up. Jason hadn't even realized Levi was there—he mostly came and went at Isabelle's side, visiting the guardhouse only when necessary. But the topic this evening applied to him, as well. He'd been assigned to guard Princess

Isabelle, then they'd fallen in love. "It depends on the relationship between the two of you. Are your intentions toward the wedding planner honorable?"

"Yes." Jason could confirm that much. He couldn't say what the future held, but he knew for certain he didn't want to hurt Ava, only to comfort her and maybe even make her smile.

"Then I don't see any problem," Levi concluded.

Grateful as he was for Levi's absolution, Jason couldn't let the issue go that easily. "I want to be certain I'm interpreting the policy fairly for everyone, while upholding the honor of the royal guard."

"If you'll recall," Galen spoke up again, "you told me not to get involved with Ruby."

"Yeah," Linus noted quietly beside his friend, "but you still kissed her when you weren't supposed to."

The tips of Galen's ears turned red, and he elbowed Linus.

"That's precisely what I'm talking about. The policy isn't clear," Jason affirmed.

"So clarify the policy," Titus said, as though the answer could possibly be that simple.

"We'll have to work on that. In the meantime, all of you have work to do. We have a royal wedding in three days." Jason nodded and headed for the door. The situation was close enough to settled for now, and he had more pressing matters to attend to. But the question would undoubtedly come up again, especially if he wanted to be involved with Ava. He didn't know what she might have to say, but he'd become increasingly certain he did want to be with Ava.

She might argue with him about it, but her kiss had told him how she really felt. It was enough to convince him. He was ready to fight for her.

* * *

Ava's heartbeat kicked up a notch when she spotted the shadowy figure lingering near the doorway of the palace-wall apartments. Though they were inside the safety of the palace campus, and Ava had so far been safe inside those walls, her life had been threatened too many times recently for her not to feel frightened.

She reached for her phone, realizing as she did so that she'd turned it off before her last meeting to avoid any rude interruptions in front of the royal family. At the same moment, she drew near enough to recognize the uniform the man wore.

Royal guard.

Ava walked toward him, faster now, studying the man's face. Her heart grew hopeful and then happy as she recognized Jason in his captain's uniform. In spite of her embarrassment at the thought of facing him again after their kiss, she couldn't help smiling as she approached him.

Jason grinned back at her.

"What are you doing here?" she called out as she approached.

"You said you were booked until ten. I tried to call your phone to arrange to meet—"

"I had it turned off."

"So I gathered." He shrugged. "So I thought I'd meet you here, but you're half an hour late."

"The meeting went long." Ava reached his side, hesitated for a moment over whether she should hug him or shake hands or give in to the urge to kiss him on the spot. Instead she pressed her thumb to the print reader until it glowed green, deactivating the lock and allowing her into the building.

"I'm sure you had a lot to discuss." Jason held the

door for her as she stepped through. He followed, giving the door an extra tug to be certain it had latched shut securely.

Ava headed toward her apartment door. "They wanted to know the latest about the situation. Of course, since Alexander has so many friends in the guard, and since he's the head of the Lydian Army, he's already learned about every development."

"Alex has top-level security clearance," Jason confirmed. "The only person allowed to keep secrets from him is the king."

"The remaining question is whether they'll be allowed to ride in the open carriage from the cathedral back to the palace." Ava paused in front of her door and looked up at Jason, still stinging from her apology to the royal couple. "I told them that for safety's sake, they ought to reconsider it."

"How did they take it?"

"With grace." Ava unlocked her door. "I could see Lillian felt disappointed, but she insisted we must do everything we can for safety's sake. I just felt awful making the request because it's my fault. I promised her the wedding of her dreams, but it's because of *me* she can't have it."

Jason stepped after her into the apartment and touched her shoulder with his hand, imparting comfort she hadn't realized she was craving. "It's not because of you. It's because of the killer who's after you. That's not your fault."

Ava blinked up at him. In her heart, she wanted to believe his words were true, but she still felt guilty. She felt the same way about abandoning him to face his men alone after they'd witnessed the kiss. "How did things go after I left?"

"With...?"

"With your men who saw our…" She looked at his lips and recalled distinctly what they'd felt like pressed to hers. She wanted to feel that again, but they had so much to discuss, and it was already late.

Jason took a step backward and ran his hands through his hair. "Yes, that. I'm afraid it's all very complicated. The royal guard has a policy against improper behavior between guards and their charges."

"You broke your own rules?" Ava felt even worse. "And all your men witnessed it?"

"It's never been clearly defined what constitutes 'improper behavior.'"

"I should think kissing would make the list if anything did."

"That was the interpretation I'd favored in the past."

"What do you mean?"

"I mean I've specifically instructed my men not to become romantically involved with the women they guard. And then I did that very thing."

Ava could see how conflicted Jason felt about what he'd done. "You could tell them it was my fault, that I kissed you—"

"I kissed you, Ava." Jason stepped closer again, so close Ava could smell the faded scent of his aftershave. "I'm not going to deny it. I'd like to do it again."

In spite of the guilt she felt, Ava couldn't help smiling.

Jason grinned back at her, and for a moment she was certain he would try to kiss her, but then he sobered. "It's late. Kissing you at headquarters might not be entirely improper, but kissing you in your apartment would be. I haven't even told you the reason I needed to see you."

Ava felt her smile fade. He hadn't waited half an hour outside her apartment hoping for a kiss? Of course not. There was still a killer at large. "What did you need?"

"Do you have any pictures of Tiffany? If Dan's story is correct and she's here looking for you, then we need to find her."

"I should be able to find some pictures for you." Ava crossed the room to her computer and turned it on. "But we've only ever seen a man in a Mariners cap. How do we know Tiffany is in Lydia?"

"We don't know it." Jason leaned over the back of her desk chair as Ava sat down to search for pictures. "That's the other things I wanted to ask you." He paused.

"Hmm?" Ava prompted once she'd finished typing and waited for her search results to appear.

"Do you have any pictures of your father?"

"My dad? Why?" She turned in her chair and looked up at him.

Jason cringed, obviously not wanting to answer, but speaking the words anyway. "We considered him a possible suspect in the beginning. He hasn't been in his office all week—I've called and asked for him every day since you were attacked. I've yet to hear anything that might clear him, not unless we can prove Dan's story is correct, which might never happen. You said your father is of similar build to the man we saw in the security footage asking for you at the gate."

"Yes, but that was Dan. He admitted that much himself."

"But the man at the security gate was of similar build to the gunman on Dorsi."

Ava realized what Jason was getting at. Though she hated to think it possible, her father might be trying to kill her.

Jason continued, "Does your father ever wear a Mariners cap?"

"Yes. Plenty of men in Seattle do. And yes, he and

Dan are both of average height and build. Dan spilled soda on his slacks at our house once, and my father lent him a pair of his pants to change into. They're the same size—but it's a common, average size. It doesn't prove anything."

"I know it doesn't. And I pray to God your father is innocent, but for all we know he could be working with Tiffany. Or Tiffany could be completely innocent and Dan's story an elaborate ruse. Or it could be something else entirely, a jilted vendor, an old client whose marriage went bad, blaming you for letting them get married in the first place. Until we know who's after you and have that person in custody, I'm not taking any chances or exonerating any suspects."

Ava found the pictures and printed them off, handing them over to Jason silently, her heart too heavy to speak.

"Thank you." He took the pictures, but barely glanced at them, all his attention on her face. His gray eyes welled with unspoken things, but Ava knew they were both far too tired to discuss anything more that night. And they had several busy days ahead of them.

Jason left with a quiet goodbye, and Ava locked the door after him.

FOURTEEN

Jason found Ava in the palace ballroom, ending her meeting with the orchestra who'd be playing for the wedding reception on Saturday.

"How'd it go?" he asked when she spotted him in the doorway and approached with a worried look on her face.

"Well, actually." In spite of her positive words, she still eyed him warily. "The Sardis Metropolitan Orchestra played for Isabelle's wedding as well as several other engagements I've coordinated. They're ready for Saturday night. Between them and the household staff, they don't even need me here."

Jason felt relieved to hear it. Given the situation, he'd already considered the possibility of asking her not to be there—for the start of the reception, at least. But that hadn't been the reason for his visit.

"So what's up?" Ava asked. "You didn't just pop by to hear the orchestra."

"I forwarded the pictures and names to the Lydian travel authorities."

"And?"

Jason pulled out the paper he'd kept rolled, almost out of sight, in his hand. "They sent me this."

Ava gasped at the security images, the time and

date stamp in the corners indicating the man had come through the Sardis Airport the previous afternoon. "That's my father."

"He flew in under his own name. No attempts to hide behind an alias."

"But if he just arrived yesterday..."

Jason guessed what she was thinking—the same thing he'd thought when he'd received the message. "The airport has no record of a Douglas Wright arriving or departing at any other time in the past year. This is the one time he's flown in under his own name."

"But he could have come earlier using an alias?" Ava studied his face as she guessed what he was getting at.

"He could have. Or he could have arrived by boat, or flown into a neighboring country and crossed the border by car. We can't rule out that he wasn't here earlier, but we do know for certain that he's arrived."

"There's no doubt that's him." Ava's voice swelled with an emotion—possibly fear—as she looked at the pictures again. "But what is he doing here?"

"I don't know. I can tell you he's been away from his office for several days, far longer than it takes to fly here, even assuming flight delays and missed connections. It raises my suspicions." Jason clamped his mouth shut before he voiced what any of those suspicions were. Reviewing the photographs with his men, they'd brainstormed plenty of theories, including that Douglas Wright was the gunman, that he'd sneaked into Lydia previously and only now made his arrival known—but for what purpose, they couldn't say, unless he was hoping to build an alibi.

And since none of those theories had any evidence to support them, Jason saw no reason to distress Ava further. He'd wanted her to see the pictures, partly so she could confirm the man in the picture was indeed her father and not a doppelgänger flying in under the man's name. And partly so she'd know what he knew and wouldn't be caught by surprise if her father suddenly showed up.

Which Jason feared the man might soon do. After all, Doug Wright's only connection to Lydia was his daughter, Ava. But the man had been in the country for nearly twenty-four hours and had yet to attempt to contact her.

What was he up to? Was he involved with his wife's murder? Given the size of Kathleen Wright's life-insurance policy, the man had stood to benefit greatly from her death, though the insurance company had apparently stalled on the payout. Which led Jason to the painful question he didn't want to have to ask.

"Ava?" He took her hand and glanced down the hallway to make sure they wouldn't be overheard. "Do you have a life-insurance policy?"

"I—I think I do. I always did. My parents opened one when I was young. To my knowledge it still exists, as long as my father has continued to pay the premiums." Her voice cracked as she spoke.

Jason pulled her against his shoulder, hating that he'd had to ask such difficult questions. "I didn't want to consider your father a suspect. I still don't. But given that he's just arrived in Lydia and you didn't invite him—"

"I haven't spoken to him since my mother's death. I can't fathom why he'd be here, not for any good reason."

"We'll do our best to get to the bottom of this. We don't know where he went once he left the airport, but my men are watching for him, just as they're watching for Tiffany and, of course, anyone wearing a Mariners baseball cap." He cleared his throat. "I do have some good news—or what I hope you'll consider good news."

"What's that?"

"I was puzzling over how to get the royal couple from the cathedral to the palace safely. We can put the rest of the wedding party and the royal family in the armor-plated limousines, but Lillian had her heart set on a horse-drawn carriage."

"I've been pondering the same question," Ava admitted. "I'm told there are catacombs under the cathedral. Do any of them lead to the palace?"

"Not that I'm aware of. Not in any sort of direct, easily accessible route, no. And I'd hate to use the catacombs for such a large event. They're supposed to be kept a secret, though of course the royals and the guards know about them. Besides, if the prince and his fiancée will agree to my idea, we won't have to resort to such an extreme measure."

"What's your idea?"

"Well over a hundred years ago—in fact, I believe it was in the same era as the assassination attempt on Queen Victoria that you brought up the other day— the reigning Lydian monarch took proactive measures against assassination attempts and ordered a bulletproof carriage. When bulletproof glass was invented, the carriage was retrofitted with windows large enough for the passengers to be seen waving to their subjects while still being protected from gunfire."

"That's a fabulous idea, Jason, but the wedding is in two days. We can't possibly have such a thing built—"

"We don't have to." Jason squeezed her hand. "The carriage still exists. It's in the museum of military history right here in Sardis."

Ava's eyes widened. "But it's a museum relic. Does it even still work?"

"We can have the glass checked and replaced—that

should be possible in two days' time. Sardis has a fabulous glass shop. They did quite a bit of bulletproof work for us following the insurgent coup last summer. And the carriage should be fully operational. All we have to do is hitch up horses to pull it. The pair who were going to pull the open carriage should have no trouble making the switch. This model is a little heavier—"

Ava cut off his words by practically leaping up at him, pulling down his face and planting a kiss on his lips.

He kissed her back, wrapping his arms around her and relishing the feel of her before he self-consciously pulled back and looked around to be sure they hadn't been spotted. The hallway was empty. "So you approve of my idea?"

"I love your idea. I promised Lillian the wedding of her dreams. Thanks to you, she might still get it."

Jason beamed down at Ava, delighted that he'd brought a smile to her face in spite of everything else that was going on. "I hope so."

Ava led Prince Alexander and Lillian out through the back courtyard doors. Jason had called to say the carriage was ready for royal inspection. The new windows had yet to be fitted, but he wanted the royal couple's appraisal before he proceeded with the update.

"What's the surprise?" Lillian asked as they stepped outside and looked around.

"Watch the vehicle gates." Ava pointed just as the gates swung open.

A pair of matching gray steeds stepped through, pulling the rounded coach, its domed top sparkling in the sunlight.

"It's a Cinderella carriage," Lily gasped. "But I

thought you said we'd have to ride in bulletproof vehicles."

"Darling, I believe it *is* bulletproof," Alexander noted, clearly recognizing the carriage from the museum.

"It is—or it will be, once the windows are replaced with newer glass. We don't want to take any chances. Do you like it?"

As she spoke, the horses came to a stop in front of them, and the footman hopped down from his perch behind the vehicle to come around and open the door.

"I love it. It's perfect!" Lillian let the footman help her inside, and Alexander stepped in after her.

"Take it for a spin," Ava instructed them. "Let me know if we need to replace the springs."

Jason stepped to her side as she spoke. "It sounds like Lillian approves," he noted with a smile.

"I'm so glad she does. Your idea was inspired."

"I had another idea I hope you'll approve of."

"What's that?"

"Dye your hair brown."

Ava hadn't been expecting him to suggest anything of the sort. It took her a moment to absorb what he'd said. "But all the vendors recognize me because of my hair. That's part of why I dyed it red in the first place—to make me easily visible."

"I don't want you to be easily visible."

The horses pranced a wide turn along the loop at the end of the courtyard and pulled the carriage to a stop again in front of them. The footman hopped down to help the royal couple disembark.

"Think about it?" Jason's voice softened. "I know it sounds extreme, but I'd do anything to keep you safe."

Ava met his eyes and saw sincere affection simmering there. Not trusting her voice, she simply nodded, waving goodbye to him as she stepped toward the royal couple. There wasn't time to discuss his suggestion further. She was always busy in the last two days before any wedding. Given that Alexander was a prince and the media had arrived en masse to cover the event, she had to make sure everything was as perfect as it could be.

The fact that someone was trying to kill her complicated things even further.

Jason arrived at the Sardis Cathedral early the next morning with a team of his men. The wedding rehearsal wouldn't begin until later that afternoon, followed by a dinner for the wedding party back at the palace. The wedding party would travel by armored limousines, including the royal couple. The carriage was still in the shop and wouldn't be ready until the next day.

But before anyone arrived, Jason and his men would do a thorough sweep of the cathedral. He'd arranged for the Sardis Police Bomb Squad to meet them later with their dogs. He wasn't about to take any chances, not with lives—especially Ava's life—in danger.

The cathedral was every bit as familiar to him as the palace. He could picture the layout of the entire floor plan, including the subterranean crypt. If anything looked out of place, he and his men would spot it.

Decorating crews had been working on the cathedral for the past two days, draping twinkle lights and tulle, placing candles ready to be lit. Everything was in place except the flowers, which would arrive early the next morning. Jason already had a team assigned to make sure no one sneaked in while the florists were at work.

At all other times, the building was to remain locked. He positioned guards at the front and rear entrances to make certain nothing was disturbed. They'd been in place in rotating shifts for most of the week. He'd taken every precaution he could think of, and yet Jason couldn't shake the fear that it wouldn't be enough.

He met the bomb squad near the rear doors and assigned his men to accompany them through the building. Just as he stepped after one of the teams to shadow their work, his phone rang.

"Captain Selini," he answered.

"Douglas Wright is at the main palace gate." The transmission of Oliver's voice broke up as he spoke, making it difficult for Jason to be sure of what he'd heard. Realizing the thick cathedral stones were probably messing with his signal, he stepped outside into the back alley and small rear parking area where several news vans were already parked. Fortunately he didn't see any sign of their crews—they were probably around front or interviewing locals for their insider perspectives.

"Douglas Wright?" he repeated. "Ava's father?"

"Yes. He came asking for Ava—"

"Is she in a secure location?" Jason could make out the words much better now, though he didn't like what he was hearing.

"She's inside the palace, meeting with the reception crew. Paul and Sam are watching her. They've been informed of the situation, but I've instructed them not to tell her just yet—and to keep her from leaving the building, if possible."

Jason appreciated Oliver's apt understanding of the situation, including his assessment of Paul's and Sam's likelihood of keeping the wedding planner from leaving if she'd made her mind up to go anywhere. He'd agreed to let her come to the cathedral for the rehearsal, but only while he was at her side. "Is Doug Wright armed?"

"They're performing a pat down right now."

"Can you detain him? Or transfer him to my phone so I can speak with him?"

"He's agitated. He's scuffling with them." Oliver sounded like a ball-game announcer calling plays. "I'm watching everything on the security screen. What's that? He tripped Milos. He's running. Elias is after him."

Jason held his breath. He could guess what the outcome would be. Elias had already passed retirement age, but the faithful royal guard had insisted on serving at least until the recruits from the army were properly trained. With Milos down, there was every likelihood Ava's father could escape.

At the same time, Jason couldn't let them leave the gate unguarded. "Dispatch more guards to cover the gate."

He heard Oliver do just that. Men could reach the gate from headquarters in seconds if they ran. Jason had full staff in place, and even the men who hadn't been assigned to the wedding shift had volunteered to work double shifts. Manpower shouldn't be a problem, but Jason hadn't expected to need extra men at that gate.

"They're at the gate. Milos is up—they waved him on. He's running."

"What now? Where is Doug Wright?"

"He's beyond the range of my cameras. I'll try to get Elias on his earpiece."

Oliver's voice became faint as Jason heard him addressing the guards who'd been stationed at the front palace gate. Jason prayed his men would detain Ava's father. He couldn't imagine why the man would approach the gate only to run away. Was it a ruse, an attempt to pull the guards away from their posts so an accomplice could sneak inside?

"They lost him," Oliver said with defeat. "He had a car."

"Was a driver waiting?"

"No. He drove off. Elias was too far behind to stop him, and by the time Milos reached them, it was all he could do to take down the plates."

"Run the plates."

"It's a rental."

"Of course it is. Find out who rented it and get back to me. I'll finish here. Don't let on to Ava what's just happened. I'll tell her when I get there shortly." Jason winced as he ended the call, already dreading what this new complication might mean and how Ava would react to it.

She'd handled everything so far with grace and poise—but then, she was a wedding planner. It was her job to remain unruffled no matter what went wrong. Even when gunmen had infiltrated the palace grounds during Duchess Julia's titling ceremony, Ava had kept the reception flowing smoothly, so that only a few irate guests had discovered they were locked down inside the ballroom.

Ava was highly skilled at holding everything together on the outside, even when she was falling apart inside. He realized that now that she'd let him see past her armor. But behind her poised facade she was terrified—and not just for her safety and everyone else's. Every time he'd had to call into question the motives of someone she'd loved and trusted, he'd watched her deflate a little, taking the blow and recovering quickly, though she'd never quite bounced back completely each time.

All these deceptions had taken their toll on her. Jason wasn't sure how much more she could handle, especially without faith in God to comfort her. He'd been praying more and more, not just for her physical safety, but also for her spiritual well-being. It hurt him to see her hurting. When she found out her father had come looking for her, it would only hurt her that much more.

And yet he had to tell her. She needed to know what had been happening, or her father might surprise her the next time, and she'd be too shocked to respond. Ava deserved to know. She would insist on knowing if she suspected anything had happened.

Jason headed back inside to let his men know he was going back to the palace a little early. He wasn't looking forward to this conversation and the hurt it would cause Ava, but he couldn't put it off. The wedding would take place the very next day. All the pieces Ava had so carefully laid out were ready to fall into place.

But what about the pieces the killer had put in place? Would they fall in due time, too? And would they take Ava with them this time?

FIFTEEN

Ava saw Jason approaching and glanced back down at her schedule, checking the time to make sure she hadn't missed anything. She excused herself quietly from the meeting, which was nearly over anyway, and met Jason near the doors.

"You're supposed to be at the cathedral," she reminded him. "Did you find something?"

"The cathedral looks clear. The dogs were just finishing their search."

"So why the visit?" Ava would have liked to tease him about not being able to stay away from her irresistible self, but she wasn't in a joking mood, and something about his expression seemed to indicate he didn't have good news to share. Uneasy fear raised goose bumps along her skin.

"Your father came to the front palace gate looking for you. When the guards tried to pat him down for weapons, he ran."

Ava closed her eyes, processing this new development. When she found her voice again, she met Jason's eyes and found comfort there, enough for her to find her voice. "What does it mean?"

"I don't know."

"How long ago?"

"Less than half an hour."

Ava looked up at the ceiling a moment as she tried to evaluate this new development. "I don't know what to do."

"There's not much we can do. Everything is in place for the wedding. Your father drove away in a car rented out yesterday under his real name. Considering that he rented the car without using a fake name, I instructed Oliver to ask all the local hotels if they've let out any rooms to a Douglas Wright. I imagine most of the hotels have been booked full well in advance of the wedding, but he has to be staying somewhere."

"You should circulate Tiffany's name, as well."

"Yes. Oliver included her name with his request, along with an image of a Seattle Mariners baseball cap."

"I'm sure the hotels are all very busy with the crowds in town for the wedding."

"Yes, but they tend to respond quickly to our inquiries. We only ask questions when security is at stake, and none of the hotels want any problems, at their hotel or anywhere in town. The insurgent coup last summer nearly killed our tourism industry. If it hadn't been for the royal weddings, we might never have bounced back."

Ava felt a reluctant smile tug at the corners of her mouth.

"What is it?"

"You make it sound as though these weddings have saved the tourism industry."

"Yes, they have," Jason insisted, looking a bit surprised that she hadn't known. "Ava, many people in our kingdom depend on tourism for their livelihood. By creating beautiful weddings, you've restored their jobs and their way of life."

In spite of his glowing words and the ardor with which he spoke them, Ava couldn't feel happy. "If the killer strikes tomorrow, that would ruin everything—not just for me and the royal family, but for all those hardworking—" Her voice caught, the awfulness of it all too much for her.

Jason squeezed her hand, letting go of her fingers to rub her back, and she leaned against him. "We'll get through this all right. Everything is going to work out."

"How can you say that? You can't make that promise when you don't know what will happen."

"I believe God is watching over us."

Ava wanted so much to believe his words were true. She'd have given anything to go back to the days when she'd truly trusted that God would keep her safe from all harm. But she'd learned otherwise the hard way. "Where was God when my mother died?"

She waited, hoping Jason would know the answer. But instead of offering her reassuring words, he remained silent. Compassion simmered in his eyes, but he had no words of hope to offer her.

Of course not. There weren't any.

She shook her head, feeling foolish for daring to hope. "I need to be going. I have another appointment shortly, and I really ought to touch up my face."

Friday evening, the wedding party assembled in the palace courtyard to travel to the cathedral for the rehearsal. Jason almost didn't recognize Ava from the back, but then she turned to face him with uncertainty on her face, and he realized instantly what she'd done. "You dyed your hair brown."

"It's my natural color. We didn't have time to add highlights. Do I look awful?"

Jason assessed her appearance. Instead of styling her hair stiffly upright, she'd left it loose, styled in curls that framed her face. "You look gorgeous, Ava. You look more like you."

"Like me?"

"In the picture on your desk."

"Oh." Her face fell slightly. "That was my engagement picture. I cut Dan out of the picture and kept the rest. Is that silly of me?"

"I'm glad you did. It helped me to realize there might be another side to you—a side I wish I'd known about long ago."

Ava gave him a thankful smile. "I really must give everyone their final instructions."

"Go." Jason squeezed her hand, then stood back as Ava directed the cars out of the courtyard in order without missing a beat. She was so good at what she did. He realized how truly blessed the kingdom of Lydia was to have her. How blessed he was to know her. He'd never learned the answer to the question his mother had prompted. How long would Ava be staying in Lydia?

He didn't suppose she'd be ready to answer that question until the killer who was after her was caught, but Jason knew he didn't want her to leave. It would take some work to clarify the Royal Guard Code of Honor to accommodate the honorable love his guards felt for the women they were involved with, but Jason now understood, thanks to Ava, just how important it was to make those clarifications. He didn't want anyone to misunderstand his love for the wedding planner.

Ava trotted back to his side. "We're in the last car." She slipped into the backseat, and he climbed in after her.

While Ava sat beside him silently and their armored car lined up at the rear of the queue, Jason debated bring-

ing up her question of faith again. He didn't want to push
her too far for fear he might push her away, but at the
same time, it pained him to know she didn't feel that God
was with her. He didn't like to see her hurting when he
knew God had the power to comfort her—if only she'd
open her heart to that possibility.

But before he could speak, his earpiece buzzed to life.

"This is Detective Varda from the Sardis Police Bomb
Squad."

"Yes, Detective Varda, go ahead." Jason recognized
the man's name from working with him before—his dog
had picked up the scent from the explosive residue on
the street after the bomb went off in Ava's car. Jason had
asked the SPBS to return to patrol the perimeter with
their dogs during the rehearsal. They'd been happy to
oblige.

"My dog picked up a scent near the front corner of
the building and followed it behind the cathedral. There
was a man in the parking lot. My dog ran at him, the
same way he would anyone carrying the scent he was
following. But before my dog caught up to him, the man
jumped into one of those TV vans parked back there.
They drove away."

"Did you get a good look at him?"

"Sorry, no. He had too much of a head start. But the
van had to navigate around another van, and I got a
pretty good look at the driver."

"Can you identify him?"

"Her. She looks like the picture you've been circulating—Tiffany Sterling? I'm not one hundred percent
certain it was her, but from what I saw, she looked the
same."

The limo had reached the front stairs of the cathedral.
It was time for Jason to escort Ava inside, but he held her

hand, preventing her from exiting until he was sure Tiffany wasn't still around. "Which way did they van go?"

"Toward the arterial highway. They turned north and headed out of town. That was the last I saw of them."

"Good. Thank you. Can you inform the others of what you've seen and file a description of the van with my office?"

"Sure thing."

"Thanks. We're here now. I'll be inside the cathedral." Jason nodded to Ava to exit, but she hesitated.

"Which way did who go?"

"Someone who looked like Tiffany and an unidentified man. They were lingering in the back parking lot, but they headed out of town. Don't worry. Now that they've seen them, neither my men nor the police will let them near here again."

Ava offered him a wan smile, which he figured was the best he could hope for, under the circumstances. Tiffany—or whoever had been driving the van—was still one step ahead of them. Until the royal guard got the upper hand, Jason didn't figure there was any reason for Ava to smile.

The rehearsal went as smoothly as any Ava had ever performed. Had it not been for the constant threat of death hovering over her, Ava would have been delighted. Instead she could barely muster a smile as she congratulated the royal couple and dismissed everyone to head back to the palace for the rehearsal dinner.

"You'll be joining us, won't you?" Lillian asked.

"I'll be a little late, I'm afraid," Ava apologized. "I'm going to do a final check of everything here, and then I'll follow after everyone's safely arrived."

Although she'd purposely tried to play down the

safety aspect of her plans, Ava watched as the meaning of the word registered with the soon-to-be princess. The simple fact was, Ava wasn't comfortable traveling the streets of Sardis too closely to the other royal cars. From the moment Jason had informed her of the likelihood that Tiffany had been staking out the cathedral in advance of the rehearsal, Ava had felt almost jittery, certain at any moment she'd see Tiffany lurking around the next corner.

She wished she could tell herself her fears were silly, but given the circumstances, the threat was all too real.

Lillian thanked her and headed out with the others. Normally Ava would have seen them off, but she didn't want to present a target, not with so many innocent people around. Instead she turned to Dom Procopio, the deacon who would be officiating over the ceremony the next day.

"Thank you so much for helping everything go so smoothly this evening." She shook his hand as she spoke. "I found your scripture reading very meaningful."

The old deacon smiled. "Alexander and Lillian selected the passage from Ecclesiastes, chapter four, but it's always been one of my favorites, especially verse twelve."

"'A cord of three strands is not easily broken,'" Ava quoted, then admitted, "That verse has always confused me. All the previous verses speak of two people, but suddenly, at the very end, the two change to three."

"Ah." Dom nodded. "You've hit upon the key to the whole passage. I don't want to give away my message for tomorrow, but since you've already picked it out, I'll tell you. The two, of course, are the loving couple who stand by each other, support and protect each other through everything. One alone is weak. Two together are

strong. But only with the third are they unbreakable."
He beamed as he spoke.

Ava nodded, though she still didn't understand. "But
who is the third strand of the cord?"

"The third strand of the cord—the One who makes
them unbreakable—is God."

Ava heard a noise behind her and turned in time to
see a shadow in the form of a man, moving toward her
from the darkened rear of the sanctuary. She startled and
just managed to stifle her scream to a yelp, recognizing
Jason as he moved into the circle of light under the last
illuminated fixture at the front of the sanctuary.

"I'm sorry," the captain apologized quickly. "I thought
you knew I was here."

"I did," Ava confessed. "I'm just so jumpy tonight."

Deacon Procopio had already moved toward the rear
hallway that led to his offices. "You two have a good
evening," he told them as he left.

"You, too! Thank you again," Ava called after him.
Then she turned her attention to Jason, squeezing the
hand he offered her, grateful not to be alone in the vast,
echoing building—and especially glad Jason was the
guard at her side. "All clear?"

"So far. They'll tell me if that changes. The limousines are heading out. Are you ready to go?"

"I'd like to wait to leave until everyone has safely
arrived at the palace. I called ahead and made arrange-
ments for the palace staff to begin serving the rehearsal
dinner without me." She took a deep breath as she explained, "It's just not worth the risk for me to be seen in
the open in proximity to everyone else—not when the
palace staff is perfectly capable of getting through the
salad course without me."

Jason smiled. "That makes good, prudent sense."

"I'm glad you agree, because I think we should do the same thing tomorrow following the ceremony."

"But isn't the wedding reception vastly more complicated?"

"It is," Ava admitted, "but everyone knows their jobs. They can start without me, and if there's any questions, I'm only a phone call away."

"We'll plan on that, then," Jason agreed, meeting her eyes with an expression that seemed to indicate he had more he wanted to say.

"What is it?" she asked when he remained silent.

"I couldn't help overhearing your conversation with the deacon."

"Oh? About Ecclesiastes?"

"Yes. And it reminded me of the question you asked last evening—where was God when your mother was dying?" Any trace of a smile had fled from Jason's face. Instead his eyes held compassion and sympathy. "I've been pondering that question ever since."

"And?" Ava asked in a whisper. She'd secretly hoped he would come up with an answer, even though she felt it was impossible.

"Have you looked at the great stained-glass windows of this cathedral?"

"Yes. They're magnificent." Ava had long admired the stained glass, but she didn't see what that had to do with her question. Perhaps Jason hadn't been able to answer it after all.

But he led her down the aisle to the darkened rear of the sanctuary, where light from the sinking sun outside poured vibrantly through the windows. Jason explained, "The images on the stained glass date back to the centuries when a large percentage of the population didn't know how to read. The windows told the gospel story with pictures instead of words." He stopped in front of a particularly moving image of Mary weeping over the slain Christ.

Ava couldn't help feeling the emotions depicted in the picture. The loss so closely mirrored what she'd felt upon losing her mother so horrifically.

"Growing up," Jason began in a strained voice, "I thought this was just a picture of Mary and Jesus. Only a few years ago did someone point out to me it's a family picture." He gestured to the dark clouds that loomed behind Mary, their stained-glass forms outlined by crisp lead lines, detailed shading sending an impression of soft rain falling from the clouds.

"Do you see?" Jason asked in a whisper.

"Is it God?"

Jason nodded. "He's weeping for His Son." Jason's voice grew heavy as he wrapped his arm around her shoulders. "I think that's where he was when your mother died. He was watching over you, weeping with you."

Tears threatened to fall from Ava's eyes, but she blinked them back. "Why did God let it happen?"

"He can't change free will. Whoever killed your mother chose evil. That was their choice. God didn't force them to do the right thing. He let them choose, even though it broke His heart."

The tears Ava had been holding back fell freely then. "I hate it," she sobbed. "I hate it that she's dead."

"So do I. If I can presume to speak for God, I think God hates it, too. I know He hates evil, and that's what her death was." Jason pulled Ava tight against him as he spoke.

Ava wrestled with the words that welled up inside

her. "I've been mad at God for a long time," she admitted, "but it doesn't help. It doesn't bring her back. Nothing can."

Jason whispered, "I think God wants to comfort you, if you'll let Him."

"But I've turned my back on Him for so long." She blushed, admitting the truth. "I yelled at God. I was angry."

"Wouldn't God rather have you yelling at Him than not talking to Him at all?" Jason offered her a hopeful smile. "You've yelled at me an awful lot in the past. That doesn't change my feelings for you."

Ava looked up at him for a long moment as Jason's words sank in. He hadn't specified precisely what his feelings for her were, but based on his tenderness toward her and his protective care, he cared for her far more than she deserved. She'd yelled at him—done her very best to push him away and been dreadfully mean—but he still cared for her.

Was it possible God still loved her, too, even after she'd turned her back on Him for so long? Ava gripped the end of the nearest pew and bowed her head while Jason rubbed her back. "Pray with me." She knit her fingers through his. "Pray for me."

Together they prayed until the heavy pit in Ava's heart dissolved into lightness. She looked down at her fingers linked through Jason's. Through her tear-blurred eyes, it was difficult to see where his fingers ended and hers began. They were like strands of a cord, knit together, not easily broken.

"I think," she admitted finally, when all her tears had been spent, "I'm finally strong enough to face whatever is going to happen tomorrow."

"You are?"

"Well, not me alone," she admitted, holding up their joined hands. "Three strands together—you, me and God."

SIXTEEN

For all of Ava's newfound confidence, Jason feared the worst the next day. None of the local hotels had admitted to having Douglas Wright or Tiffany Sterling among their guests. And yet Jason was nearly certain both of them were in the city somewhere.

And one of them, or both together, were almost certainly still plotting to kill Ava. And just like the day before when the bomb-squad dog had chased one of them, they could show up at any moment, without warning.

He couldn't hope they'd run away so quickly a second time.

Jason had done everything he knew to do. He'd taken every precaution short of postponing the wedding itself.

That would have been next to impossible and completely inadvisable. A crowd of invited guests poured from vehicles well ahead of the ceremony start time. His guards looked better than respectable in their formal uniforms and polished shoes as they checked the invitations of every guest who arrived. Guests had been forewarned to bring photo identification with them. Fortunately most of those attending Alexander's wedding were used to the procedure, which had also been required at Isabelle's ceremony.

They'd roped off the back parking lot for the royal limousines, sending the television vans off to a lot several blocks away. The SPBS patrolled with their dogs far beyond the range of the guests. Jason could only pray their visible presence would be enough to keep the killer away.

An hour passed, and most of another, before Jason's earpiece buzzed. "The wedding party is lining up to depart from the palace."

"I'll be right there," Jason assured them. It was a short drive and usually an uneventful one. Jason had parked a royal-guard motorcycle around the block from the cathedral. He reached it quickly and made his way to the palace, glancing down each side street he passed, alert for any out-of-place television vans or any sign of trouble.

A shiver passed through him in spite of the bright sunshine. He felt almost as though he was being watched. Surely those who were after Ava were nearby, waiting for the right opportunity to make their move. From the standpoint of the would-be killers, the royal wedding was the perfect opportunity to strike. Not only did the event force Ava out of hiding, but unlike the day before when there had only been the wedding party to keep track of, today the throngs of guests had the royal guard stretched thin.

Jason couldn't imagine the killers letting this opportunity slip by without seizing it. He feared at any moment they'd make their move, but still he arrived at the palace without incident, just as Ava ushered the first members of the royal family into the waiting limousines. The wedding planner's pale yellow gown with its fluttery sleeves was a shade lighter than Lillian's cheery buttercup bridesmaid dresses and of a slightly more subdued style, though it flattered her fit figure perfectly. Jason found he had to force himself to look away from her and focus on watching over the royals.

Elaine, the queen mother, helped her husband, the former king, as he stooped to climb into the vehicle. The once-strong leader had been frail ever since he'd taken a bullet defending his daughters in the wake of the insurgent uprising. He was no longer up to ruling the country, but his eldest son, King Thaddeus, performed that job with grace.

Thaddeus and his very-pregnant wife, Queen Monica, stepped into the next car with their son, Prince Peter. The queen was due to have twins in another month, with the various Sardis newspapers taking sides over whether the babies would be boys, girls or one of each. To Jason's knowledge—and he had some of the best intel in the palace—no one knew the gender of the babies, save possibly the royal family themselves, though none of them had whispered a thing about it to anyone.

The princesses Isabelle and Anastasia took the next car, along with their guards, Isabelle's husband, Levi Grenaldo, and Anastasia's fiancé, Kirk Covington. The father of the bride joined them in their limousine.

More members of the wedding party followed. Prince Alexander's groomsmen included Titus, the royal guard the prince credited with saving his and Lily's lives in the deserts of North Africa. Jason didn't begrudge the guard his position—in fact, he considered it helpful to have a trained man so close to the wedding party. Titus had even insisted on wearing an earpiece so he could use his position to the greatest advantage.

Finally Lillian Bardici's closest friends, who were serving as bridesmaids, poured from the castle surrounding the bride in her long, white gown. They held her train and her long, flowing veil to keep it from touching the ground and delicately tucked everything around her in the limousine before climbing into the car after her.

Jason assessed the progress of the elegant wedding party. When they were all ensconced in their assigned vehicles, he stepped over to Ava's side and offered her his elbow. "Ready?"

"I guess." Ava placed her hand on his arm and let him lead her. "Can you feel me trembling?"

He could. Her hand shook so hard he had to focus on keeping his arm still. "You're not usually nervous before weddings, are you?"

"Usually only a little." She paused as he opened the door to the sedan that would take them to the cathedral. "But usually no one's trying to kill me." She ducked inside, and Jason scooted in after her, nodding to Paul to proceed.

Since the thought had occurred to him before, Jason confessed, "I'm impressed with how well you're holding together, given the circumstances."

She cast him a wry smile. "It's my job. Weddings are full of chaos and uncertainty and things going wrong at the last moment. My job is to absorb all those blows, fix whatever I can and keep a level head so the bride and groom can enjoy their day."

Jason grinned at her explanation of her duties, realizing only as she made her explanation that their job descriptions weren't all that different—not really. Perhaps that was another reason they'd clashed so much—they were both trying to achieve the same thing, but without working together. He'd be sure to rectify that in the future, assuming he could convince Ava to stay in Lydia. And his new recruits could learn a great deal from this elegant, courageous woman.

But for the moment, Jason needed to focus on the

wedding. According to the plan he'd gone over with his guards the evening before, Ava and Jason would arrive first, hopefully before anyone realized the wedding party was on its way. Paul would stop in front of the steps to the cathedral and come around to open the door for them. With Paul blocking visibility on one side and Jason on the other, the two of them would escort her into the building.

Once they were safely inside, Paul would climb back into the car and drive away, clearing the way for the rest of the royals to arrive, with Ava poised to receive them. Prince Alexander was already there, waiting with Dom Procopio in his back study.

The tricky part, of course, would be getting Ava safely inside the building. Though barricades kept the crowd and media at bay, Jason had seen the masses gathered just beyond the velvet ropes—a throng of people so thick a killer could easily blend in among them. Besides the ground-level spectators, there were people watching from the windows and balconies of all the nearby buildings, including the U.S. embassy across the street from the cathedral.

The killer could be anywhere.

The short car ride felt painfully long, though the sedan didn't once stop. Finally they reached the front of the cathedral. As planned, Paul put the vehicle in Park and trotted around the back side to open Ava's door. She stepped out between the armored guard and the armored car door.

Jason slid out behind her, swept one arm around her waist and led her up the stairs with Paul close by on the other side. Alexander's officers from the army lined the steps on either side, their bayonets pointed skyward, their white suits nearly blinding in the bright sunlight.

The guards at the top of the stairs pulled one door

open as Ava neared the top of the stairs. Jason ushered Ava through and stepped in after her, his eyes taking a moment to adjust after the bright sunlight outside.

He quickly identified all those standing nearby. Guards—Jason recognized each one of them.

They'd made it safely through the first step.

How many more remained? Rather than allow himself to think about the long day that stretched before them—and the many longer days that stretched after as long as the killer remained at large—Jason focused on the next step. The guards would allow the distinguished arrivals through one by one. Music already flowed out from the sanctuary to the large front narthex, where the wedding party would arrange themselves.

Jason stood at Ava's side as she expertly handled all the splendor of the formalities. Once Lillian was inside and safely tucked away out of sight with her bridesmaids in a small parlor between the narthex and the fellowship hall, Ava used her walkie-talkie to instruct Dom Procopio to send Prince Alexander out to escort his parents up the aisle.

The queen mother let her frail husband hold tight to the prince's arm, while she supported him from the other side. They progressed slowly up the center aisle as the orchestra played deep in the apse, behind the chancel, its notes filling the ancient sanctuary high to the vaulted ceiling. The musicians themselves were all but completely hidden from view by the massive candelabras and floral displays that had transformed the chancel into a veritable Garden of Eden dominated by white lilies and lilies of the valley.

Once the prince's parents were seated in the front pew, Alexander took his place at the front next to the deacon, and Ava began sending up the members of the

wedding party in pairs. First, Lily's friends with their
escorts, then Alex's sisters, Isabelle on Levi's arm, Anastasia with Kirk Covington. Finally with King Thaddeus serving as his brother's best man, the king escorted
Queen Monica, pregnant and glowing, her bouquet of lilies perched above her swelling baby bump, to the front,
where, as planned, the queen was given a spot near the
queen mother and former king in the front pew.

But instead of sitting, Queen Monica remained standing. At Ava's signal, the music changed, swelling to the
opening notes of the bridal march as Lily emerged on
her father's arm last of all, as beautiful as her name-
sake flower, which she carried in a massive bouquet that
trailed nearly to the hem of her gown.

The queen mother rose and the rest of the congregation followed suit. At the front of the sanctuary, Prince
Alexander's face beamed with emotion as he caught his
first glimpse of his bride in her wedding gown.

Jason looked down at Ava, who stood just out of sight
of most of the congregation, peeking through a gap between the last of the three sets of double doors at the
rear of the sanctuary. Her attention was fully focused
on the bride's progress up the aisle. Lillian looked lovely
in her wedding gown. But in Jason's eyes, Ava was the
real beauty, selflessly devoted to the happiness of the
families she served.

What was it she'd promised her brides? To give them
the wedding of their dreams?

Suddenly Jason realized he wanted nothing more than
to give Ava that very same thing. What would she look
like in a flowing white gown, holding flowers, walking
toward him as he stood by Dom Procopio's side? She'd
be breathtaking. But would Ava even be interested in
marrying him? She'd never mentioned what her feelings

were or even whether she intended to return to the United States once her term of service had ended.

"Ready?" Ava looked up at him.

Jason blinked, so lost in thought he had to refocus his attention on the present. Lily had reached the front of the sanctuary. He and Ava were now to climb the back spiral staircase that led to the balcony. From there they'd oversee the rest of the service. Realizing he needed to remain alert and not allow his thoughts to drift off again, Jason led the way up the stairs, checking first around every bend to be certain no one lay in wait for them.

They reached the top safely, and as Jason had expected, based on the successful rehearsal the day before, the rest of the service went smoothly, save for the bride nearly losing her voice to happy tears as she repeated her vows to the prince. Ava stayed in the balcony as the recessional began to play, using the bird's-eye vantage point to oversee everyone's exit.

When the bride and groom reached the rear of the sanctuary, Ava contacted the men below, who escorted the pair into the parlor again while the rest of the wedding party and the guests gathered outside.

Finally, with Ava overseeing everything from the balcony through an opened panel of the great stained-glass window that overlooked the front stairs of the cathedral, the pair of horses arrived pulling the bulletproof carriage, and Ava used her walkie-talkie to let the bellmen know it was time to ring the ancient church bells.

Musical cacophony filled the air as the bells rang out from the high tower above. At their signal, the bride and groom stepped out together.

Cheers erupted all along the street, along with flashbulbs and cloudbursts of white paper confetti as the prince and his bride descended the stairs and climbed into the carriage. The horses obediently stepped forward at the driver's signal, and the carriage rolled away toward the palace. In its place, limousines queued up to collect their passengers.

Ava oversaw it all, staying in contact with the men below until the last of the dignitaries had reached their cars and the guards sent up word that the wedding party had arrived inside the safety of the palace gates.

Only then did Ava turn her attention to him. "We can leave once all the guests are inside the palace gates. It shouldn't be long now."

"Let's head downstairs." Jason held out his hand, grateful when she clasped her fingers around his as he led her back to the main floor. From there, the plan was for the two of them to sneak out through the back-alley door, signaling Paul to meet them with the car, timing his approach and theirs so the sedan would spend minimal time idling in the alley. They didn't want the vehicle to sit there long enough to draw attention.

Guards met them on the main floor. "The last of the guests have left the building."

"Good. Do a final sweep of the building to make sure all the doors are locked and latched, then head for the palace. We'll need you there."

"Yes, sir."

Jason led Ava to a back hallway. He contacted Paul as they walked.

"I'm two blocks away," the guard informed him. "I have a straight shot to the alley door. Let me know when you're ready."

Since they were alone in the back hallway, and since Jason knew it would be many more long minutes before all the guests made their way to the palace, he decided it was his best opportunity to ask the question that had been burning inside him throughout the entire ceremony.

"What are your plans once the weddings are over?"

Ava smiled up at him. "I'm going to take my shoes off and soak in a warm bath."

"That sounds relaxing." Jason cleared his throat. "I was thinking more about what you're planning to do once Anastasia's wedding is over. The royals have you booked through that event—but what do you see yourself doing then?"

Ava nibbled her lower lip as she met his eyes in the dimly lit hallway. "They had asked me to stay on as the royal-event coordinator. I've not yet given them an answer, and in light of the threat against my life, well…" Her voice faded and she looked down at the floor.

Jason's heart pounded as he guessed what she might be about to say. But even that didn't prepare him for hearing the words.

"I think it would be safer for everyone in Lydia if I went back to the States tomorrow."

"No."

Ava looked up at him, her eyes wide with surprise.

Even he hadn't expected to voice his disagreement out loud, but the word had escaped like a breath from a physical blow.

"What?" Ava looked confused.

"I don't think that will solve anything. You'll still be in danger. I can't protect you there. I can't go with you."

"My presence here endangers everyone—the royals, innocent bystanders, the guards, you."

"Me?"

"You were hit by a car protecting me. You've been at my side every time I've left the palace. It's not safe for you. I can't—"

To Jason's chagrin, her words were cut off by a transmission to his earpiece. "All of the guests on our list have safely arrived. The way is clear."

"We're clear," Jason informed Ava.

"Let's go."

"We don't have to be in a hurry—" He hoped to finish their conversation, to convince her to stay before she entertained the notion of leaving for even a moment longer.

"I feel terrible about being absent from the reception this long. We can talk in the car, if you like."

"Yes. Of course." Jason pressed the button that allowed him to speak to Paul via earpiece. "We're ready for you."

"I'll be there in twenty seconds."

"We'll be waiting."

Ava stepped toward the door ahead of him. She seemed eager to escape their conversation, which worried him. Why was she so intent on leaving? What were her feelings toward him? He knew he didn't want to lose her. Even if her killer was caught and she was safe to return home without any threat of danger, he still didn't want her to leave.

But she seemed completely intent on going.

"Ava." He stopped her, placing one hand over hers as she gripped the slam bar that would unlock and open the rear alley door. "Wait until Paul arrives with the car." Then, pressing the talk button, he asked Paul, "Are you here?"

"Waiting on cross traffic. I thought most of the crowd had left, but—"

While Paul's voice buzzed in his ear, Ava, either misunderstanding that Paul hadn't yet arrived or simply eager to escape their conversation, leaned against the slam bar just far enough to disengage the lock, though the door remained shut.

"Ava," he chided her, pulling back up on the bar.

But he was too late. In that brief moment, someone on the other side tugged the door outward. Sunlight poured in through the crack.

Jason pulled the door back, tugging on the slam bar with all his strength while Paul prattled on in his ear-piece about how slow the traffic was moving.

The party on the other side tugged the door open toward the alleyway. They clearly wanted in.

"Who is it? Do you need something?" Jason asked, praying inwardly that the person on the other side wanted in for innocent reasons. Maybe a guest had forgotten something—but all the guests were already at the palace.

No one answered his question. The person simply tugged all the harder on the door. Jason braced his feet and pulled back with all his might, moving the latch to within a hairbreadth of engaging with the lock.

A massive tug on the other side pulled it open an inch or more—not far, but far enough that whoever was trying to get in was able to lodge a stiff object in the opening, preventing it from going closed.

Jason reached for the object, prepared to push it back, when he recognized exactly what it was.

The barrel of a handgun.

In one swift move, Jason wrapped an arm around Ava's waist, practically plucking her from the ground as he lunged back down the hallway toward the ninety-degree turn and the protective cover offered by the thick stone walls. He prayed they'd make it out of sight before the door opened behind them.

Shots rang out behind him as Jason all but threw Ava ahead of him around the corner and dived after her. He heard at least two sets of footsteps landing hard on the stone floor as their pursuers ran after them.

"Gunmen in the cathedral," Jason yelled into his ear-piece as they ran down the next length of hallway toward the church offices. "Repeat—gunmen are in the cathedral."

SEVENTEEN

Ava slowed her steps as they reached the end of the hallway. Her instincts told her to try to escape the building, to reach the guards who were surely still outside, somewhere in the near vicinity, but the hallway that led to the front doors had its start near the door where the gunmen had burst in. They couldn't go that way.

The only other route was to go through the sanctuary.

"This way." Ava pulled Jason through the small back door that led into the chancel. The front of the sanctuary was filled with flowers and extinguished candles, the scent of their smoke still lingering in the air. The room was dark, with only faint shadows of sunlight penetrating the stained glass.

They shuffled forward hesitantly. Ava glanced down the back of the sanctuary. The orchestra's chairs and music stands still cluttered the space in front of the organ pipes. The forty-eight floral displays, each of them twice as tall as Jason, were to be taken around to the local nursing homes and hospitals the next day, but for now they loomed like fragrant giants bowing in the empty church.

Jason whispered, "They're right behind us. We have to run for it, but stay low."

They hurried down the chancel, toward the carved

wooden knee wall that separated the front of the sanctuary from the pews beyond. Ava sized up their options. The center aisle would be the fastest route to the front doors, though it would put them in clear sight. The side aisles stretched so very far away on either side, with thick columns all but blocking their path at even intervals.

But the columns would offer them cover.

They passed the knee wall and Ava turned to head toward the side aisle.

"The center is faster." Jason pulled her in that direction. "Running targets are difficult to hit," he assured her.

Trusting him, Ava followed. They darted alongside the knee wall, headed for the wide shallow steps where the wedding party had stood throughout the ceremony. From there they could reach the aisle and make their way to the front of the sanctuary and out the front doors to safety.

"Stay low," Jason whispered, his words nearly buried by the sound of a door slamming open behind them—the same door they'd entered through.

Jason pushed her down, out of sight next to the knee wall, and huddled over her as an all-too-familiar voice echoed through the sanctuary. He held his gun ready in his other hand. Ava could only assume he'd wait to shoot until he had a clear shot, rather than risk giving away their position.

"Where did they go?" It was Tiffany's voice, sounding angry and slightly breathless.

"I don't see them now, but they came through this door. They're in here somewhere. Let's split up."

In spite of the pounding of her heart that made it difficult to hear, Ava was certain the man who responded was not her father. Good. Tiffany wasn't working with her dad.

Unfortunately whoever she was working with seemed to know what he was doing.

"Check behind all the flower displays. They've got to be hiding. They didn't have time to reach the back doors."

He was right. They hadn't had time to reach the doors—in fact, they were as far from any door as they could get, in all but the dead center of the enormous room.

Ava held her breath. Judging by the sound of Tiffany's and her accomplice's footsteps, every sound was amplified by the high-vaulted ceilings. Ava could hear the two of them making their way across the apse, checking behind each candelabra and floral display as they went, making their way closer, ever closer to the place where she and Jason crouched, hidden only by the low engraved wooden wall.

Once Tiffany and the other gunman got close enough, they'd be sure to see her and Jason crouching there. Based on the shots they'd fired into the hallway as they'd forced their way inside, Ava didn't figure either of the pair would hesitate to shoot them on sight.

Jason squeezed her arm. She turned her head just slightly. Was he giving her a signal? They didn't dare try to move. Their footsteps would echo through the room. Tiffany and her accomplice would pick them off before they got halfway down the aisle, moving target or not.

From far away, she could hear the hollow echoes in the distant narthex. Surely Jason's men had returned. Were they struggling to open the doors they'd locked behind them when they'd exited the building to head for the palace? She wondered which of them had a key, if any.

Praying silently, she willed them to find a way into the building, to step inside the sanctuary, to find Tiffany and her accomplice and capture them before it was too late.

But the distant booming died away to silence.

One set of shuffling footsteps moved closer through the floral displays. The other echoed from farther back in the apse, near the organ pipes, where the members of the orchestra had left their chairs and music stands.

Suddenly a loud clattering noise filled the chancel. Jason tugged her forward, running, ducked low, alongside the knee wall toward the other side of the chancel.

Music stands continued to fall behind them, and Tiffany berated her partner for his clumsiness. Ava thought quickly as they ran. There was another small door on the other side of the chancel, its wood the same color and style as the ancient wooden paneling that lined the front of the sanctuary. It led back to the hallway through which they'd entered the chancel.

It wouldn't take them to the front doors, but it would get them out of the sanctuary and away from the gunmen, for a short while, at least.

Ava dived for the small door, throwing herself against it, stumbling through with Jason right behind her. She gasped a breath as the door swung shut behind her.

"That way!" Tiffany screamed, her voice filling the quiet sanctuary. "Through that door."

"Where now?" Ava asked, at a loss. Her wedding-planning duties had required her to be familiar with the sanctuary and the main entrances and exits, but she didn't know as much about these back hallways or the other secrets of the vast building.

Jason glanced down the hall. "We'll never make it to an exterior door from here." He tugged her by the hand down a narrow hallway that bent past the offices.

Ava wanted to ask where they were going, or if Jason even knew what they'd find at the end of the hallway, but she didn't dare speak. They rounded a bend in the hallway just as the door behind them slammed open again, and Tiffany's voice echoed down the corridor.

"They went this way!"

From the sound of the vengeful woman's voice, Tiffany must have caught a glimpse of them before they disappeared around the bend in the hall, because the sound followed them and footsteps pounded after them.

"Stay back," Jason whispered, pushing her against the stone wall behind him as he leaned just far enough around the corner to shoot. He got two shots off before the gunmen fired back.

"Aah!" Jason's gun flew wide, shot from his hand. He glanced at the fallen weapon. He'd have to go out in the open to retrieve it, and the gunman would be upon them in a moment, and obviously the man was an excellent shot to have shot the gun free from Jason's hand. It was too risky.

Jason pushed her farther down the hall. "This way." He led her to a thick door. He didn't hesitate but pushed them through it, whispering, "Stairs. Careful."

Ava could see nothing in the utter darkness. A dank chill rose to meet them as they descended by feel. Ava leaned on Jason's arm, depending on him to catch her if she missed a step in the darkness. She'd never been down this way before, but she'd heard rumors of the place and could guess where they were heading.

Cold air hit her as they reached the bottom, and she nearly stumbled over her own feet, half expecting another step down, but finding nothing in the darkness.

Jason pulled out his phone and hit a button to illuminate the screen, providing just enough dim glow for

them to see the space before them. The crypt ran underneath the cathedral for what had to be the full length of
the building, though the light from Jason's phone didn't
allow them to see nearly that far.

They hurried forward while his phone provided them
with light.

"There's a way out on the other side—the stairs come
up under the stairs to the balcony."

Ava had seen the door before, and once even peeked
inside, noted the spiral of steps descending into darkness
and quickly closed it again. She hadn't wanted anything
to do with the spooky space then, but now that stairwell
was her only hope. If they could reach it quickly, they
might be able to escape the building before Tiffany and
her accomplice caught up to them.

Jason's phone went dark again, but not before Ava had
caught a glimpse of the layout of the subterranean mausoleum. The central corridor traveled down the middle
of the vast underground space, with large chambers of
vaults on either side. These stone rooms were divided
by massive walls—vaults that contained the bones of the
leaders of Lydia long dead.

The chambers themselves hosted statues and marble
plaques, the still, human forms nearly as large as Ava
and Jason, their eyes staring blankly ahead. Ava shivered. Even in the darkness she could picture their frozen
forms, their faces almost lifelike, their hands holding
scepters or Bibles or reaching out with empty fingers
as though to grab anyone who brushed by too closely
as they went past.

Given the darkness, Ava and Jason crept forward with
their arms outstretched ahead of them, moving as quickly
as they dared without bumping into anything. Behind
them, Ava could hear the sounds of their pursuers de-

scending the steps. They'd soon be in the crypt, and Ava knew she and the captain weren't yet halfway through the lengthy underground corridor.

"Watch your step. That's the bottom," a male voice muttered far behind them.

Ava wished she could sprint forward to the stairs somewhere ahead, but if either Tiffany or her accomplice turned on any sort of light, they'd spot them in an instant and surely shoot them just as quickly. In fact, she felt a little surprised their pursuers hadn't found a light source yet.

"In here," Jason whispered close to her ear as the pair behind them muttered about needing light. The captain tugged her sideways, and they slid along a wall of burial chambers, ducking behind what felt like a large marble statue.

Faint light glowed from far down the corridor. Tiffany or her partner must have pulled out a phone. Ava realized that she and Jason were out of sight for now, ducking low as they were in one of the branching chambers. But the stone room had only one exit—the way they'd entered, through the central passage. As long as Tiffany remained in the corridor, Ava and Jason were trapped.

"What's at the other end?" Tiffany asked as the light glowed stronger, moving down the central hallway.

"I don't know."

"Go look."

Footsteps echoed, light grew stronger and then Ava watched as a man, cell phone clutched in one outstretched hand, hurried along the passageway toward the spiral stairs that opened up to the narthex above.

"There's a door," the man called back once he reached the end.

"Where's it go?"

"I don't know." Thumping echoed through the crypt. "Nowhere. It's locked."

"Then they couldn't have escaped that way," Tiffany summarized. Her light faded and returned. "These are burial chambers. Do any of them have exits in them?"

"Doesn't look like it."

"How do you know? If any of these rooms have an exit, they could escape."

Ava held her breath as the cell-phone lights dimmed and brightened while the pair ducked into side rooms looking for escape routes.

"We saw them come this way. If there's no way out, they must still be in here," the man mused softly.

"But if there's a way out, we need to find it quickly." Tiffany sounded almost frantic.

Suddenly Ava heard a musical note sounding from far too close. Jason clapped a hand against his phone, silencing it almost an instant after it began to ring.

With a sinking heart, Ava realized his men must have tried to call him—from what she'd been told, his earpiece wouldn't work deep in the cathedral because of the thick stones. He'd alerted the guards to gunmen in the cathedral. Of course they'd tried to contact him, little knowing that by doing so, they'd given away their presence to the gunmen.

"Was that your phone?" Tiffany asked.

"Nope. Yours?"

"No—it had to have been theirs. They must be in here!"

The man chuckled gleefully. "We'll find them."

"Search each room carefully, one by one. You start at that end. I'll work from this end. They could be hiding anywhere. Check all the dark corners. If you see them, don't wait for me. Just shoot." Tiffany made a grumbling sound, then muttered, "She's even harder to kill than her mother was."

Fear and sorrow clawed at Ava's heart. So Tiffany had indeed killed her mother. Dan's story had been true, his theory correct. And just as surely, Tiffany would find her. There was no way out of the mausoleum now, not with Tiffany and her partner blocking escape from either end.

The most Ava could hope for was that Jason's guards would capture Tiffany as she tried to escape the cathedral afterward—otherwise they might never realize precisely who'd killed her, and Tiffany would get away with murder.

Again.

Ava clutched Jason's arm as he held her tight against him behind the statue that hid them. He held her so close she could feel his heart beating hard, its pace almost as frantic as hers.

Regret sliced through her with cutting claws, each one a painful reminder. Jason was going to die because of her—and not just because she'd lured a heartless killer to Lydia but because he'd insisted on protecting Ava himself. He'd been too brave, too determined, too honorable. If he'd run and left her to face Tiffany alone, he would have at least escaped alive.

But of course, Jason would never do that. Her heart pinched inside her as she realized how deeply she truly cared for him. She'd realized days ago that he was a better man than her former fiancé. She'd once planned to marry Dan. Jason's personality fit her so much better, and yet she'd never even told the captain how she felt.

Truly, she'd opened her heart to him so quickly it had frightened her, and she'd been unwilling to lower her last defenses and admit how she really felt, especially when it seemed certain she'd have to leave Lydia—and Jason—to keep everyone in the kingdom safe.

She'd failed to keep him safe. Worse yet, she'd failed to tell him how much he meant to her.

The lights grew brighter as their pursuers drew inexorably closer, their lights fading in turn as they checked each chamber thoroughly and then moved on to the next. Ava didn't know how many chambers there were. A dozen, perhaps, on either side? Surely not many more than that. It wouldn't be long now.

"You might as well show yourself," Tiffany goaded, her voice impatient. "You're not going to get away. You think you're so smart. Taking all the best contracts, keeping me out of the limelight. Don't you think I noticed? But you won't get the last laugh. I'm the smartest. I'm going to win."

While Tiffany prattled on, Jason took advantage of the noise the woman made and bent close to Ava's ear, whispering softly, "When the lights dim, meaning they're both in chambers, we'll jump across the hallway, toward the right. The chambers are staggered." He fell silent when Tiffany paused.

Ava could see the wisdom of Jason's plan. True, they'd be exposing themselves to possible attack, creeping closer to Tiffany instead of farther away. But their only hope was to somehow make their way closer to the chambers she'd already checked.

They'd have to cross her path in the process. Even if she was deep inside one of the rooms, even if she continued to talk to herself, she'd surely hear their footsteps, or the other gunman would. They were only three or four chambers away in either direction.

She might see them and shoot, but she was bound to

do that anyway. This way, at least, they had some hope of sneaking past her.

It was the only plan they had—a long shot, but still, better than no shot at all. And Ava trusted Jason. She felt the same comforting reassurance that had flooded her the evening before as she'd prayed to God in the cathedral above. That had been a leap of faith.

This, though more literal, would be little different. God had caught her last night.

Would God catch her again?

She didn't have time to wonder. First Tiffany's light, then the other gunman's faded as the two stepped into chambers to search.

Jason squeezed her hand, maneuvered them both deftly around the statue to the doorway, and together they leaped toward the doorway across the dark corridor and a little to the left. The light from the searching gunmen provided just enough illumination for Ava to see the faint outline of the doorway to the chamber and duck inside, with Jason darting in on her heels.

As she'd feared, both Tiffany and her partner heard the sound.

"That's them!" Tiffany cried.

"There they go!" her partner shouted at the same time.

The lights grew brighter as the pair spoke. Ava crouched low behind the solid stone wall while Jason shielded her from above as the sound of gunfire erupted in the hallway.

Shots echoed, ricocheting off the stone walls, the noise too fiercely loud in the enclosed space for Ava to even attempt to count how many shots had gone off. Four? Six? They had fired simultaneously.

And then silence.

Ava had no idea what was going on in the corridor just

beyond them, but she knew she and Jason were likely going to die.

"I love you," she whispered, praying those words wouldn't give away their location, but knowing she'd gladly give her last breath to speak them while Jason was still alive to hear.

"What?" The captain looked down at her—the lights from their pursuers' cell phones still glowed, unmoving, from the hallway, providing just enough light for Ava to make out Jason's movement in the darkness.

"I love you," she whispered again.

One cell phone light went out.

Then the other.

"I love you, too, Ava." He leaned down and kissed her.

Ava kissed him back, unsure why Tiffany was waiting to strike, but glad for this last moment with Jason, at least.

"Have you checked down here?"

"I thought I heard gunfire."

Men's voices echoed from the stairs, followed by hard soles pounding down the stone stairs. "There's a light switch somewhere. It's very tricky to find. There."

Bright light flooded the crypt. Ava buried her face against Jason's shirt to shield her eyes from the sudden brightness.

The men who'd entered gasped.

"Bodies!"

"Who?"

She heard people running as she put together the clues.

Bodies?

The gunfire—Tiffany and her accomplice had both fired. They were the only other two in the crypt, weren't they? So *bodies* must mean…

"It's Tiffany Sterling. I recognize her from the photos the captain circulated. She's dead."

"This one's dead, too. Looks like they shot each other."

"But where is the captain?"

Jason cleared his throat and stepped forward. "Is it safe to come out?"

"Captain!"

The pair of guards looked pale with relief. "And Ava!"

Their smiles didn't fade as Jason pulled her out of the chamber after him.

"You're both all right?"

"By God's grace, yes," Jason answered.

Ava glanced down the hallway and saw the pair who'd pursued her nearly to death. She shuddered quickly and looked away, hiding her face in Jason's arm, shivering in the cool of the crypt.

"I should give you my statement," the captain acknowledged, "but I also need to get the wedding planner over to the reception. They expected her some time ago, and with the eyes of the world watching the Lydian wedding—"

"Go." The guards gestured toward the stairs, assuring him, "We can process the crime scene. Get moving."

Jason tested his earpiece as they climbed the stairs and finally made contact when they reached the main floor. "Paul, do you have that car for me?"

Ava listened closely but couldn't hear Paul's response. However, she could tell from Jason's reaction that the guard had reported something unusual.

"It's okay. You're sure he's not armed? I think it will be all right. I'll ask her. We'll meet you in the alley."

"What is it?" Ava asked when Jason finally stopped talking and looked down at her. She tried to read some indication of whether his news was good or bad, but he seemed to be struggling to sort out that difference himself.

"It seems," he began slowly as he led her down the hallway, back toward the door through which the gunmen had entered, "when I reported gunmen in the cathedral, my transmission wasn't clear. There was some confusion among the guards about where I was, and when they couldn't get in the locked doors, they were all but convinced I needed their help somewhere else entirely."

They reached the back door and Jason paused, staring for a moment at a bullet hole in the far wall, which Ava was nearly certain hadn't been there until the moment Tiffany and her accomplice had forced their way in.

"As they were debating it, a man ran up to them and insisted he'd been tracking Tiffany and the gunman for the last two days. He claimed to have seen them enter through the alley door. It was only then that my guards decided to force their way back in and met us in the crypt."

Ava's mouth dropped open. "I'm so glad he convinced them. But who was it?"

As she asked the question, Jason opened the door to the alley, and Ava blinked at the man who stood next to Paul, leaning against the royal-guard sedan, waiting for them.

"Your father."

EIGHTEEN

Ava took a few hesitant steps toward the car.

Douglas Wright looked just as uncertain as he stepped toward his daughter.

"Daddy?" Ava's voice cracked as she approached him, blinking back tears that fell soon enough anyway.

"I hope you don't mind," the American pastor said softly.

"Mind?"

Paul looked uncomfortable with the way the two of them gawked at each other. The guard jumped into the conversation. "If it hadn't been for this man, we wouldn't be here. He saw the gunmen enter the building. Without him, we wouldn't have had a clue."

Ava finally seemed convinced, by either Paul's words, her father's hopeful expression or the prompting of her own heart. She stepped toward her father, arms extended, and gave him a hug.

"I'm sorry for everything," Douglas Wright said softly. "I didn't know—for so long I was in such a stupor of shock I couldn't even think about what had happened. Then Dan tried to reach me. I refused to speak to him. I was afraid he wanted to get back together with you again. I was afraid he'd hurt you. I deleted his emails without reading them, until he sent one with a subject line claiming he knew who'd killed your mother."

Jason listened closely to everything the pastor said. It all fit Dan's story—and the current situation.

Ava's father continued, "When I read the email, I didn't want to believe it. I tried to reach Tiffany. I spent three days trying to track down her car, visiting every junk lot in Seattle before I found it. She'd patched the bumper with duct tape, but when I peeled it back, it matched the missing piece."

"Tiffany killed Mom," Ava acknowledged softly.

"I'm afraid she did. I turned over the evidence to the police. They put out a warrant for her arrest, but nobody could find her. Dan had warned me Tiffany might target you next. So what could I do?" Doug extended his arms and looked down at his daughter. "I came here. I wasn't sure if I should bother you or if you'd even speak to me—I didn't have your phone number or address—so I focused my efforts on tracking down Tiffany."

"But you came to the palace gates once."

"I thought you should know what was going on. But then the guards acted like I was a threat. I heard one of them say something about the killer who was after you. I got spooked and ran. I realized they knew someone was after you, but I didn't want them to think I was that person. If they put me away, I wouldn't be able to help you."

Jason felt his heart swell as Ava's father finished his story. He felt relieved that all the pieces fit. More so, he was glad to see Ava reconciled with her father. But at the same time, they'd already lingered longer than he wanted.

"We need to get back to the palace. Would you like to ride with us?"

"I'd appreciate that very much," Douglas told him,

taking the front passenger seat. Jason and Ava sat together in the backseat for the short trip to the palace.

"Do I look okay?" Ava asked, pulling a tissue from the dispenser in the center console. "I'm probably a mess."

"Allow me." Jason cupped his hand around hers. She handed over the tissue, and he dabbed away the still-moist tracks her tears had made on the way down her cheeks. Then he wiped away the last of the smudges around her eyes. "You look perfect."

She smiled at him, a hint of mischief in her eyes, and took the tissue from him. "You've got a little lipstick," she explained, swiping at the corner of his mouth.

Jason grinned back, a surge of affection replacing the nervous beat of his heart.

When they reached the palace, Jason was relieved to find the wedding reception proceeding peacefully.

"Any problems?" he asked his men at the gatehouse.

"The prince and his bride were asking for Ava—I think they want to thank her before they leave for the night."

Jason realized that, after all their adventures at the cathedral and taking time to listen to Doug's story, Ava had nearly missed the entire reception. But to her credit as a wedding planner, she'd put all the pieces into place so well the event had gone smoothly even without her. The car pulled forward, and Jason took Ava's hand to help her from the car.

She met his eyes as she stepped out, and Jason's affection swelled inside him. Ava had told him she thought she should return to the States after the wedding—but that was before Tiffany had been stopped. Did Ava still feel the same way about leaving? Jason wanted to ask her, but the royal couple had already waited long enough.

"This way." Jason led her toward the palace doors. "Alexander and Lillian were asking for you."

"I'll wait out here," Doug volunteered.

Jason gave Paul quick instructions to make sure Doug was comfortable, before hurrying toward the palace holding Ava's hand.

"I hope everything is all right." Ava sounded concerned and somewhat chastened for her tardiness.

"I'm sure it is," Jason tried to assure her as he held the palace door open for her. He didn't want her to worry—she'd done enough of that in the past week already. More than that, he didn't want her to leave. Lydia needed her. He needed her.

But how did she feel now that Tiffany had been stopped?

They entered the grand reception hall, where glowing chandeliers hung low over tables filled with guests. Near the orchestra, couples waltzed on the dance floor under dimmed lights. Jason spotted the prince and his bride circulating among the guests. Prince Alexander looked up, spotted them and smiled.

"There they are," Jason said to Ava, leading her toward the newlyweds.

As they approached, Lillian flew at Ava, beaming. To Jason's surprise, the bride embraced the wedding planner.

"You're finally here! I was worried about you."

"You shouldn't be worried about me—not on your day." Ava squeezed her back. "I'm fine. Everything's fine. Didn't the guards tell you?"

"They said the situation was resolved, but until I saw you with my own eyes, I couldn't help fearing they were only downplaying what had happened." The bride gave Jason an accusatory glance. "They do that sometimes, you know, so the royal family won't worry." Her accusation ended with a happy giggle. "I'm so glad to see you're okay. I wanted so much to thank you for all you've done. Today was perfect."

"Was it?" Ava sounded pleased, but slightly less than convinced. Jason figured that made sense—her day had been far from perfect, quite possibly one of the worst in her life. He wished he could turn things around for her, and quickly.

"Oh, yes!" Lillian beamed up at Prince Alexander. "I married the man of my dreams, in the wedding of my dreams."

"I'm so glad." Ava's face lit up with a broad smile.

Alexander tugged his wife in another direction. "Look, darling, the prime minister."

Jason nodded at the prince as he led his wife over to speak with the distinguished guest. Ava bustled through the crowd, monitoring the waitstaff and the orchestra, speaking with several of her contacts before she finally stood back and surveyed the room, looking satisfied as she sipped a glass of punch he'd grabbed for her.

"Everything in order?" Jason asked.

"Remarkably, yes—even without me."

"It's a testimony to your skill as a wedding planner."

"I can't take all the credit."

"But you can enjoy it a moment, can't you?"

Ava looked a little taken aback. "What do you mean?"

"Can you dance?"

"Of course I can dance, but—"

Jason took her emptied glass and set it on the tray of a passing waiter. "Dance with me."

"In front of your men?" Ava looked around at the uniformed guards who stood at regular intervals around the perimeter, besides those who were part of the wedding party. "I thought you weren't supposed to—"

"We're addressing that." He took her hand and led her toward the dance floor.

"You are? When?"

"Starting now." He turned to face her on the dance floor, placing one hand at her waist.

"I didn't realize you danced."

"Of course I do. Royal guards are renowned for their grace and sophistication as much as their courage and strength." He smiled as they began to dance. "And besides—I have five older sisters who made me their practice dummy."

Ava giggled as she waltzed gracefully alongside him. "I can't imagine you being anyone's dummy."

They danced in happy silence for another few moments before the orchestra changed their tune.

"What's this?" Jason asked.

"Oh—it's American music. Lillian requested it."

"It's slow, but I don't think I can waltz to it."

"No," Ava admitted. "You're supposed to—" She blushed a bit and stepped closer to him.

Jason knew enough about American dancing from movies and television to understand. "We basically get to hold each other and sway in time to the music?"

"That's pretty much it, yes," Ava admitted, still blushing slightly, though she grinned up at him and didn't seem to mind at all having his arms wrapped around her.

"I must confess, I approve of your American tradition," Jason murmured close to her ear.

"I'm so glad. But what will your men think?"

"I'll discuss the policy with them tomorrow. They can consider this a visual demonstration. I've always tried to lead by example."

As they swayed in time to the music, Ava rested her cheek on his shoulder. Jason had so many things he wanted to discuss with her—urgent questions such as her plans for returning to America and whether her words earlier in the vault were brought on by the situation, or if she really meant them.

And if she confessed she really meant them, he had another question he wanted to ask.

But for now, Ava seemed to be enjoying herself, and that was something Jason knew she didn't often get to do. His questions could wait until tomorrow. For now, he wanted nothing more than to hold Ava close as they danced.

The next morning, after meeting her father for breakfast at the grand buffet the palace laid out for all the wedding guests who'd stayed over, Ava went back to her apartment and read through her plans for Princess Anastasia's wedding. She couldn't put off planning any longer. If Jason wouldn't let her use the island of Dorsi, she would make the royal couple understand. She trusted Jason.

In fact, she more than trusted him. She wanted to work with him on this project—very closely, if necessary—but she didn't want to argue, not the way they'd argued before. After all they'd been through together, she couldn't imagine spending her life with anyone else. Still, if she was going to stay in Lydia, she needed to do her job. Right now that meant presenting the princess's wedding plan to the captain of the guard.

Ava cringed as she printed off the papers and carried them over to the royal-guard headquarters, and prayed Jason wouldn't be upset with her. She didn't have an appointment with him, but she figured she could at least leave the papers with the dispatcher.

But the man behind the glass smiled at her when she approached him.

"These are for the captain." She slipped the papers into the slot underneath the bulletproof panel.

"Would you like to deliver them in person?" the man asked.

Surprised, and glad she might get the opportunity to explain herself, Ava asked, "Is he here?"

"He's in a meeting," the dispatcher admitted. "But I can buzz you through if you promise not to disrupt him until he's finished."

"I'd appreciate that. Thank you." Ava recognized the man behind the glass, but his words were so different from the way he'd spoken to her before. She quickly crossed the room and went through the door, following Jason's voice down the hallway, lingering just out of sight around the doorway of the conference room where he addressed his men.

"The deceased has positively been identified as Tiffany Sterling. We followed up on the hotel-room key she had with her—she and her accomplice had checked into a local hotel under false names."

"What about the accomplice?" a guard asked.

"He's been identified as a hired hit man, wanted in the U.S. for several counts of murder." Jason rapped pages against the table as he spoke. "We're considering the case closed."

"What about the wedding planner?"

"What about her?" Jason clarified.

"Is she going to have a guard assigned to her, or are you going to take care of that?"

Ava could hear the insinuation in the guard's voice,

even from the hallway. She peeked just far enough around the doorway to see Jason's face and prayed he wouldn't spot her until after he'd answered.

"Now that the threat against her life has ended, Ms. Wright is no longer in danger. However, I do believe that as long as she chooses to remain in Lydia, she will most often be traveling in my company."

An excited murmur moved through the room.

Jason continued, "That brings me to the real reason for this meeting. You men all know I've placed a priority on restoring the reputation of the royal guard. As part of that, I've strictly interpreted the clause regarding interactions between guards and their charges. In light of recent developments, I believe we need to reinterpret that clause."

"Sir?"

"I'm going to work with those guards who are most knowledgeable on the subject—Galen, Linus, Levi and Kirk—all guards who've become engaged to their charges, to craft a precise policy that will allow for love without compromising the reputation of the guard."

The murmuring around the room continued, along with clapping and other sounds of approval. As Ava watched from the doorway, one of the guards who'd transferred from the army—Titus, she believed was his name—stood and held out a newspaper.

"On the subject of the guard's reputation, I don't know if all of you have seen the news report about yesterday's wedding." Titus cleared his throat and read, "'The royal guard, which was considered a threat in the wake of the attacks last summer, has proven to be the pride of Lydia. Captain Jason Selini leads his men with dignity, and the guard contributed to the elegance and success of the royal wedding.'"

The last of Titus's words were drowned out by cheering and clapping. Ava, overcome with the knowledge that Jason was finally getting the credit he deserved for all his hard work, couldn't resist the urge to let out a whoop of approval.

The men quieted quickly, and all heads turned her way.

Too late, Ava realized her voice hadn't blended in with the others. She nearly ducked away, but Jason strode quickly toward her, pulled her inside the doorway and planted a kiss on her lips.

Surprised by his sudden enthusiasm, she nonetheless recovered quickly and kissed him back. "Congratulations, Captain," she said as the men clapped and cheered.

Jason ended the kiss by nuzzling her lightly. "What brings you here?"

Suddenly unsure about the wedding plans she carried, Ava held them out, biting her lip as she awaited his response. She didn't want to fight with him—not now, not in front of his men. "It's the same plan you already rejected," she admitted, blushing. "If you really don't think it's safe…"

Her voice trailed off as Jason surprised her with a smile. "You're not planning to go back to the States? You'll stay and do the wedding?"

"I'll stay as long as the royal family will have me."

Jason beamed down at her with one arm still secure around her waist, holding her close to him. "I'll approve the location on one condition."

"Yes?"

"We should plan our own wedding there."

Ava felt her mouth drop open, but she wasn't entirely certain how to respond. Jason's eyes twinkled mischievously. Finding her voice, Ava asked, "What do you mean?"

"I mean you and I should get married there. I love you." Jason grinned. "I can't imagine working with you on another wedding without planning one ourselves."

"You're not afraid we'll end up fighting all the time?"

"There's no one in the world I'd rather argue with." Jason planted a tiny kiss on her cheek. "But I don't think we'll ever argue so much again, not now that we've learned to work together." He kissed her other cheek, then met her eyes. "I want to make you smile, Ava. I want to hear you laugh every day. I need you in my life."

Encouraged by his words, Ava smiled. "I think you and I can face anything together. What did that Bible verse say? 'A cord of three strands is not easily broken.' If I have you and God…" Her words trailed off as she pressed a kiss to his lips.

The men started to clap again, until one of them said, "Wait—we haven't heard her answer."

With that, Jason pulled back and raised his eyebrows inquisitively. "Do you have an answer? Will you marry me?"

Hardly believing her happiness, Ava answered quickly, "Yes!"

Jason kissed her again as all the guards cheered.

* * * * *

Dear Reader,

Ava spent a lot of time yelling at Jason, but that didn't stop him from loving her. In the same way, God loves us, even if we've spent more time yelling at Him than thanking or praising Him. Do you believe this is true?

I hope you've enjoyed reading about Jason and Ava and the kingdom of Lydia. For more information on other books about Lydia—both suspenseful and historical—visit my website, www.rachellemccalla.com. You can also find me on Facebook, Goodreads and Twitter.

Blessings,

Rachelle McCalla

Questions for Discussion

1. Wedding planner Ava Wright promises her brides the wedding of their dreams. Ava is willing to be pushy and demanding in order to make good on her promises. How do you feel about Ava's behavior? How does her behavior change when her faith is renewed?

2. Captain Jason Selini is focused on restoring the honor of the royal guard. What obstacles stand in his way? What would you have done in Jason's position?

3. Ava and Jason clash repeatedly as they pursue their separate goals. Do you think their strong feelings are the opposite of love, or is there a fine line between anger and love? Has anyone ever acted angrily toward you when, in fact, they actually care for you very much (perhaps a parent or authority figure)? How can/did you make your interactions with that person more positive? How did Ava and Jason transform their relationship?

4. When Ava's car is bombed, she is shocked and denies that anyone would specifically target her. How does Ava's attitude change as the threats against her continue? Have you ever denied something could be a certain way, only to realize later it was the very thing you denied it to be?

5. After Ava's previous engagement ended, she kept the picture of herself to remind her of what it felt

like to be loved and happy. What do you think of her choice? What does that decision reveal about her character?

6. When Jason is hit by the car, his body armor is dented, so Ava helps him remove it. In what ways does Jason, likewise, help Ava remove the "armor" she's put up around her heart? How could you tell that Ava was beginning to lower her defenses?

7. In the beginning of the story, Jason thinks of Ava as "the wedding planner." Likewise, Ava sees Jason as "the captain." When and how do they begin to think of each other on a first-name basis? What do these changes reveal about their deeper feelings? Does it make a difference whether you think of people in terms of their job or their name?

8. Ava wants Jason to approve holding Princess Anastasia's wedding on the island of Dorsi, where the Lydian kings and queens of long ago were married. What do you think of her plan? What about Jason's arguments against it? Who would you side with? Why?

9. As Jason questions the people who knew Ava in the U.S., he realizes they see her differently than he sees her. What caused the difference? Do you think it was because she'd changed or because Jason failed to see the real Ava? Or was there more going on?

10. When Ava listens to Jason interrogating Dan, she realizes her former fiancé wasn't the best match for her. But while she's thinking in those terms, she re-

alizes that Jason is much better for her. Have you ever thought you'd found the person you wanted to marry, only to realize later he or she wasn't nearly as perfect for you as you thought? What made you realize that? Do you agree with Ava that it was a good thing Dan cheated on her, so she didn't end up married to him?

11. What do you think about the relationship between Ava and her father? Do you think her anger toward him was justifiable? How do you feel about the way their relationship was resolved?

12. Jason is the youngest captain of the guard in the history of Lydia. Do you think he was the right choice for the job? How do you feel about the way he interacts with the other guards, including the new recruits? Do you feel the royal guards behave honorably?

13. Ava gave her best friend Happily Ever After, the wedding-planning business they'd built together. In light of the events between them, how do you feel about this exchange? Has a good friend ever betrayed you, even after you tried to make him or her happy?

14. Ava has been angry with God since her mother's death. Do you agree with Jason, that God weeps when people choose evil? Have you ever felt angry with God? How did you find peace again?

15. Jason insists that even though he and Ava have yelled at each other many times, that doesn't change

the way he feels about her. Neither does God love her any less. How do you feel about Jason's statement? Do you think he and Ava make a good couple? Do you think their love will last?

REQUEST YOUR FREE BOOKS!

2 FREE RIVETING INSPIRATIONAL NOVELS
PLUS 2 FREE MYSTERY GIFTS

Love Inspired®
SUSPENSE

YES! Please send me 2 FREE Love Inspired® Suspense novels and my 2 FREE mystery gifts (gifts are worth about $10). After receiving them, if I don't wish to receive any more books, I can return the shipping statement marked "cancel." If I don't cancel, I will receive 4 brand-new novels every month and be billed just $4.74 per book in the U.S. or $5.24 per book in Canada. That's a savings of at least 21% off the cover price. It's quite a bargain! Shipping and handling is just 50¢ per book in the U.S. and 75¢ per book in Canada.* I understand that accepting the 2 free books and gifts places me under no obligation to buy anything. I can always return a shipment and cancel at any time. Even if I never buy another book, the two free books and gifts are mine to keep forever.

123/323 IDN F5AC

Name _____ (PLEASE PRINT) _____

Address _____ Apt. # _____

City _____ State/Prov. _____ Zip/Postal Code _____

Signature (if under 18, a parent or guardian must sign) _____

Mail to the Harlequin® Reader Service:
IN U.S.A.: P.O. Box 1867, Buffalo, NY 14240-1867
IN CANADA: P.O. Box 609, Fort Erie, Ontario L2A 5X3

**Are you a current subscriber to Love Inspired Suspense books
and want to receive the larger-print edition?
Call 1-800-873-8635 or visit www.ReaderService.com.**

* Terms and prices subject to change without notice. Prices do not include applicable taxes. Sales tax applicable in N.Y. Canadian residents will be charged applicable taxes. Offer not valid in Quebec. This offer is limited to one order per household. Not valid for current subscribers to Love Inspired Suspense books. All orders subject to credit approval. Credit or debit balances in a customer's account(s) may be offset by any other outstanding balance owed by or to the customer. Please allow 4 to 6 weeks for delivery. Offer available while quantities last.

Your Privacy—The Harlequin® Reader Service is committed to protecting your privacy. Our Privacy Policy is available online at www.ReaderService.com or upon request from the Harlequin Reader Service.

We make a portion of our mailing list available to reputable third parties that offer products we believe may interest you. If you prefer that we not exchange your name with third parties, or if you wish to clarify or modify your communication preferences, please visit us at www.ReaderService.com/consumerschoice or write to us at Harlequin Reader Service Preference Service, P.O. Box 9062, Buffalo, NY 14269. Include your complete name and address.

LIS13R

An attack stole her memory. Can she get it back in time
to save a missing child? Read on for a preview of
STOLEN MEMORIES by Liz Johnson,
the next exciting book in the
WITNESS PROTECTION *series*
from Love Inspired Suspense.

Everything before that moment was blank.

It took considerable effort, but she pried her right eye open far enough to cringe at the glaring light wedged between white ceiling tiles. Pain sliced like a knife at her temple. She tried to lift her hand to press it to her skull. Maybe that would keep it from shattering. But her arm had tripled in size and weighed more than a beached whale. She could only lift it an inch from where it lay at her side.

Fire shot from her elbow to the tip of her middle finger, a sob escaping from somewhere deep in her chest and leaving a scar inside her throat as it escaped.

"Julie?"

Julie? She turned to look in the direction of the voice to see who else was in the room, but something plastic tugged against her nose. An oxygen mask. She didn't even try to lift her hand to adjust it, instead rolling her eyes as far as she could.

A gentle hand with cold fingers pressed against her forearm, but the face was just out of reach. "Julie? How are you feeling?"

Who was Julie? There wasn't anyone else in her limited line of sight, but that didn't mean the other girl wasn't close by.

A face—round and blurry—appeared right above her. Wide-set blue eyes shone with compassion and the same brilliance as her white smile. "I'm Tammy, your ICU nurse." Cool fingers secured the cannula back into place and brushed across her forehead.

What was she doing in the ICU? On a hospital bed in the ICU? And why had the nurse been calling her Julie?

That wasn't her name.

"I know someone who's been looking forward to talking with you. If you're ready, I'm going to let Detective Jones know that he can come in and see you. He's been waiting to talk with you for three days."

She tried to shake her head. A detective? As in a police officer? Why were the police coming to see her? What had she done?

Can Julie remember her past to save her future?
Pick up STOLEN MEMORIES wherever
Love Inspired Suspense books are sold to find out.

A new job has brought Heath Monroe to Whisper Falls.
Cassie Blackwell might just convince him to stay. Read on
for a preview of THE LAWMAN'S HONOR
by Linda Goodnight, Book #4 in the
WHISPER FALLS *series.*

As he left the garage and started down Easy Street, a jaywalker caught his attention.

He whipped the car into a U-turn and parked at an angle in front of Evie's Sweets and Eats. He pressed the window button and watched as Cassie stepped up on the curb.

"Morning," he said.

"How are you?"

Better now.

"Healing." He touched the bruise over his left cheekbone. "How's it look?"

"Awful." But her smile softened the word.

Cassie had something that appealed to him. A kind of chic wholesomeness mixed with Southern friendly and a dash of real pretty.

He hitched his chin toward the bakery. "Were you going in there?"

"Lunch. Want to come?"

"Best invitation I've had all day." The ankle screamed at the first step, causing an involuntary hiss that infuriated Heath.

Cassie paused, watching him. "You're still in pain."

"No, I'm fine."

She made a disbelieving noise in the back of her throat. "You remind me so much of my brother."

"Must be a great guy."

"The best. You should meet him."

"I'd like that."

"Come to church Sunday and you will."

With his ankle throbbing, he somehow held the door open for Cassie and limped inside a small business. The smells of fresh breads and fruit Danish mingled with a showcase of pies and homemade candies.

"A cop's dream," he muttered, only half joking.

A middle-aged woman—Evie, he supposed—created their orders while maintaining a stream of small talk with Cassie. Cassie took the lunch tray before he could and led the way to a table.

"So how bad is your leg? I mean really. No bluffing. Any other injuries besides that?"

"Just the ankle. Sprained. And a couple of bruises here and there." Bruises that ripped the air out of his lungs.

"When do you want your mani-pedi?"

Heath choked, grabbed for the tea glass and managed to swallow. "My what?"

The thought of Cassie touching him again gave him a funny tingle. A nice tingle, come to think of it. Did she have any idea the thoughts that went through a man's head at the most inappropriate times?

"You don't remember our conversation?" she asked. "Is the concussion still bothering you?"

"Slight headache if I get tired. Nothing to worry about." Then why did he suddenly have all these thoughts about a woman he'd only just met?

Is it possible Heath's found something besides work to focus on? Find out in award-winning author Linda Goodnight's THE LAWMAN'S HONOR, on sale in March 2014, wherever Love Inspired® books are sold!